ARCHIE THE LAND ROVER

By Christopher Mahoney

1. ARCHIE

It was 1992 and Archie was in despair, there had been good times, particularly when he was a new motor, but not now, he had fallen into the grippers of a bodge it and shift it car dealer. Archie had passed through the grippers of a number of car dealers, which wasn't so bad when he had been in his prime. After all, back then, the most that he needed was a wash and a good polish, in those days he had a full service history! Archie always had many admirers whilst he stood on the garage forecourt, all primped and polished. Quite often he displayed the highest price, he used to feel so proud, but as they say, pride comes before a fall. As it happened, he thought this particular saying was a load of old nonsense, why after all shouldn't you be proud if you are top dog so to speak, give yourself a pat on the back, or roof in Archie's case. No, the real problem was age, his parts didn't always work as they should, this may have been due to over use when he was younger, but you can't turn the clock back. In any case, if you've got it, you should flaunt it, make the most of it while you can.

So here he was, the motor dealer was a young wheelman, he might improve with age and experience, you've got to give a fellow the benefit of the doubt after all. In the mean time however, Archie had been subjected to a very half hearted rub down, with some quite abrasive and uncomfortable wet and dry paper, a quick mask up, and then blasted not so carefully with dark blue paint. It wasn't even the right colour, he was supposed to be Land Rover marine blue, this was Ford ambassador blue, it just wasn't right, and Archie here was being a bit of a snob, Ford, not exactly Land Rover territory is it!

Now Archie here had known quite a few Fords, they were ok in a cheap get the job done sort of a way. Archie even had some Ford friends, although he tended to keep that quiet in the good old days in the golf club car park. The problem was standards, even the best golf club car parks seemed to be filling up with black cabs and plumbers vans, what had happened to all the Jaguars and Bentleys? More to the point, the vans were quite often Fords, and the black cabs mostly had Ford engines. Archie had even heard a scandalous story that Ford were trying to buy Land Rover! At least it wasn't the Germans, that really would be the end.

In the meantime, getting back to the matter of standards, Archie's paint job just did not cut the mustard. Archie being a Land Rover of advanced years, had a good deal of quality galvanised parts. This is zinc plated steel, which does not rust, therefore it does not require paint, it should be left naked in all its dull grey glory. Well not today, ambassador blue paint had been blasted over everything, it looked ok at a distance, but it wasn't going to last. As for Archie's interior, it looked like a herd of Rhino's had recently partied down inside, his seats and door cards were in a terrible condition, Archie needed a good hosing out at the very least. Then his interior paintwork was currently an eyeball wrenching bright blue, Archie had long since decided, his current custodian must have been on amphetamines whenever he got the paint brush out!

Archie was terribly embarrassed by his condition, he was after all special, a one off, well one of twelve actually. To be absolutely concise about this, he was the second of twelve pre-production 109 V8's. Archie had stories to tell, he had been to places, had experiences that regular production land lovers can only dream of. Now he was in the possession of Spud the second hand car dealer, this fellow plainly did not realise Archie's importance. Archie was royalty in land rover circles, he had a three and a half litre V8 which had Buick in its blood line, twin Stromberg carburettors, oversize twin leading shoe front brakes, permanent four wheel drive, none of this part time stuff. Constant velocity joints in his front axles, a locking differential in his gearbox, a chassis which was specific to his type, Archie knew he was a benchmark, with his restrictors taken out he could hit the ton! Archie had noticed though, any wheelman who went that fast, would hold his steering wheel very tightly with their grippers, stop in-taking air through the hole in their front piece, expose their front piece cutters whilst jamming them tightly together, and open their light receptors very wide! He couldn't understand what all the fuss was about.

But that was then, this was now, Spud just didn't understand Archie's capabilities. He had taken Archie into a muddy field, but didn't engage Archie's locking centre differential, this is operated by a small vacuum switch, almost hidden away on top of his transmission tunnel. Archie put up a very poor performance, onlookers shook their heads and turned away! If Archie could have gone to the Blast Furnace at that ignominious moment, he would have, he even had to be rescued by a Japanese four wheel drive! The shame was almost too great for Archie to bear.

So now here he was, parked up on a grass verge in Buckinghamshire of all places. Archie had been to the Namibian Desert in the early days, strutting his stuff with a genuine Land Rover test driver and crew. He was important and knew it, the very future of Land Rover depended upon Archie and his twelve comrades! Some of them didn't make it, driven to destruction in the quest for Land Rover perfection. You needed balls of steel to be a pre-prod Land Rover, Archie had them in abundance, in his wheel bearings, differentials, gearbox, transfer case. Name a part and Archie's steel balls, ok, sometimes rollers or even taper rollers, were there! Now Bucks, not the currency you understand, the place. Archie had recently been flashed, not a publicity shot like the old days. No, this was a well known motor publication, Archie had seen the company logo on the flash operators pedal pumper covers. He was up for sale, the princely sum of one thousand eight hundred and fifty petrol tokens, his forecourt a grass verge! A few weeks passed with very little interest from any potential custodians. Archie noticed that the hand written sign in his window was now one thousand five hundred petrol tokens, Archie felt very cheap, how could this possibly be? He commanded respect on the road, the riff-raff would get out of his way, wheelmen, generally speaking, paid many petrol tokens to have custodianship for a few years.

Archie had to admit that he had his faults, his gearbox sang like a Tenor who has inadvertently sat on a drawing pin, and he hadn't been serviced for two years. What could Archie do but wait. A few potential wheelmen had turned up, kicked his tyres and gone for a drive, unable to get his diff lock to work, they made excuses about his thirsty V8, his noisy gearbox, and left. One afternoon, Archie was awoken from his slumbers by the slamming of a car door. Parked facing him was a mark 1 Ford Granada estate, Archie knew the type well, brash and showy, a thirsty 2.5 litre V6 engine, soft suspension, useless off road. But wait, Archie knew a few Fords, they were a hardy bunch, could take a bit of stick, Archie quietly liked Fords.

The Ford wheelman had a fairly lengthy conversation with Archie's car dealer. After much opening of doors and bonnet, rolling underneath, prodding and banging Archie's under-parts, the Ford wheelman was in Archie's drivers seat on a test drive. Archie was impressed, this fellow drove with gusto, gave his V8 a bit of a workout, got some air and petrol mixture in Archie's V8 lungs. Archie noticed that this fellow spoke very loudly at all times, could it be that his hearing wasn't quite up to scratch? This could be a good omen, maybe this wheelman wouldn't notice the high octave at which Archie's gearbox operated. Then, much to Archie's surprise, the fellow told Spud that the diff lock didn't work because the vacuum switch was sticking, if spud could fix it, he would buy Archie. At last, a new wheelman, and here was a fellow used to vehicles that like a drop of petroleum spirit, a Ford V6 owner. They all drink petrol like its going out of fashion, and he is plainly deaf, a pre-requisite for the custodian of an old Land Rover, this was excellent, Archie couldn't believe his luck. A few days passed and the Ford owner returned, an exchange of petrol tokens took place and Archie was on his way.

2. OPTIMISTIC

Archie hoped he wouldn't embarrass himself with any unexpected ailments, he was only to well aware that he hadn't been very well looked after of recent years, a full service history was a thing of the past. All was going well, Archie had noted that the wheelman's Ford Granada was of 1974 vintage, two years older than he was, it was in good condition, which must have been due to wheelman's efforts, this Archie hoped bode well for him. Then it started to rain heavily, Archie knew that his trusty V8 did have an Achilles heel. His big cooling fan tended to suck any passing water droplets in through his radiator, then blow them over his electrics, which was not good for his sparks. Now this wasn't the fault of the water droplets, they were completely innocent of any malice, all they wanted to do was find a nice warm place and be vaporized. The problem, of which Archie was only to painfully aware, was his coil. It didn't cause him any physical pain you understand, he is made of ferrous and non-ferrous metals, which generally speaking have no pain threshold. This was a mental thing, Archie after all had a consciousness and feelings, a Land Rover should not be stopped by a little splash of water. But Archie's coil was old and past its prime, its sparks were weak, it should have been changed years ago, it was all part of the neglect!

Archie could feel the misfire starting, first one cylinder and then another, Archie was slowing and losing power, his new wheelman was dropping down through the gears, fourth to third to second. Wheelman was pumping the throttle and dipping Archie's clutch, trying to get his V8 to spin up, then it happened, Archie's engine cut out. Wheelman managed to get Archie half onto a grass verge so as not to block the road, now he had Archie's bonnet up, and feared the worse. Archie's V8 had stopped with a rattle, Archie was fully aware that the rattle was not a problem, but wheelman had spent some time on the journey, sucking his front piece cutters, and tapping at Archie's oil pressure gauge with a gripper digit.

Now Archie's V8 runs very low oil pressure, but at high volume, he is made that way, the problem is the dodgy oil pressure gauge, which shows no oil pressure when Archie is hot. Archie could see that his new wheelman was despondent, he could see that shuffling walk, felt that completely unnecessary kick to his front nearside tyre. The matter was not helped by the fact that it was hammering down with rain, wheelman was looking very soggy. Fortunately salvation was at hand, a man with a yellow van was parked nearby at the entrance to a horse show, wheelman was a member of this trusty organisation, a very sensible arrangement. Particularly for a wheelman taking to the highways of this green and pleasant, but occasionally very wet land, whilst at the wheel of an older and more mature motor. Archie was pleased, this wheelman had foresight, planned for the unexpected. Not that Archie was in any doubts about his abilities, he was after all a Land Rover, a machine of stout and simple heart. The clue though lay in the name, Land Rover, he needed to be fettled regularly, his parts old and new oiled and regularly greased, this unfortunately was not the case. Archie was no longer bomb proof in the breakdown department, wheelman being a member of that virtuous get you out of a pickle club, would be advantageous.

Archie's bonnet was opened, the yellow clad wheelman prodded and poked around Archie's venerable V8, gave his electric's a good soaking with water dispersant spray, the friend of spanner men the world over. Archie loved the stuff, he felt the propane propellant creeping into his air intake, that for Archie was the bonus! The yellow clad wheelman turned Archie's key, his V8 heart roared into life, Archie was ready, he was pumped, he could take on anything. A one-in-one slope, three ton horse box, bags of cement and sand, he had done it before, he could do it again! Archie saw that his new wheelman was smiling, pumping the yellow clad wheelman's gripper in a hearty fashion, then wheelman walked back to Archie. He looked happy, but Archie realised that the overriding feeling was relief that Archie hadn't expired. Wheelman patted Archie's bonnet as he walked past, jumped into the drivers seat and gave Archie's throttle a good prod. Archie roared again, wheelman patted his steering wheel with his gripper, then slotted Archie into gear, and set off once again for Archie's new home.

Archie was driven for about an hour, before arriving at a yard behind a wheelman shelter. Archie realised this was temporary, as a wheelman other than his wheelman, appeared to shelter here. Pleasantries were exchanged, Archie's new wheelman waved his gripper in a friendly fashion, then left in the green Ford Granada he had seen a few days previously. Archie realised that he was the Fords replacement, he had picked up on his wheelman's conversation, the Ford was destined for a motor publication photo-shoot. Archie was saddened by this news, the Ford was a good motor, trusty, reliable, but Archie had detected oxidation in the old motor. The Blast Furnace was not too far away for the Ford, unless funds were available for welding. Archie suspected this was not the case, he had been purchased for a knock down price due to his age and poor condition. He had heard the wheelman mention four hundred petrol tokens, as the sum for which he would let the Ford go, this was a paltry sum, would lead to the Ford being purchased by another wheelman with limited funds. It was a sad and downhill slope for the old Ford, the old car knew it. Archie could tell by the settled look of the Fords rear springs, the slight rust pulling through the filler around his headlamp bezel. The two motors exchanged knowing look's, he would do his best to fill the shoes of the old car, saddened by the fate which he knew awaited the Ford. Falling into the hands of an uncaring wheelman, the abuse that would follow, the final trip to the Blast Furnace.

So it was that Archie was parked up in that rear yard for a few weeks, wheelman still had the old Ford and paid regular visits to Archie. He brought along his Lady wheelman, and four miniature wheelman on one occasion, they all climbed aboard, and Archie took his new family for a blast around the local roads. Wheelman drove with gusto, held Archie in each gear so that he could listen to the V8 song, Archie loved it. All that petrol air mixture being sucked into his heart, the power he felt through his transmission, it was like the old days. The lady wheelman and the miniatures loved it too, there was much excitement as wheelman explored Archie's capabilities, Archie liked this family, felt that his consciousness was on the upturn.

In the following weeks, wheelman measured up Archie's doors where the tops were rusted out, and the front bulkhead where it was holed, he returned with steel repair pieces which he riveted and bolted in place. Archie felt stronger and ready to hit the road, his oil and filters were changed, his universal and ball joints greased. He had been right about this wheelman, here was a fellow who would care for him and keep him fettled, maybe a new paint job and interior, Archie felt the future looked good.

3. NEW HOME

After several weeks languishing in the back yard, wheelman turned up one day without any tools, what could this mean, no more tinkering. Archie had developed a liking for the easy life tucked away in his corner, the occasional visit by wheelman to fit new parts to him. After a few words with the shelters resident, wheelman climbed aboard, gave Archie a good dose of choke and fired him up. Archie felt a sense of purpose about wheelman, this wasn't another blast around the block to clear the cobwebs, he was off to his new home.

It was a short drive, twenty minutes at most, Archie wondered what his new garage was going to be like, would it be heated? Would it have an inspection pit, maybe a car lift? No more nights of being rained on, or waking in the morning with a thick frost on his roof, Archie felt positively smug. It came as a shock, Archie should have realised at the outset, he was a budget buy, the Ford a budget sale. Archie's garage heaven hopes died when he was parked in a lay-by opposite wheelman's shelter.

Consciousness could be cruel, here he was, 109 V8 number two, parked in a lay-by on a busy urban road. Would he escape a lunatic wheelman, crashing into him whilst he was parked and minding his own business? Archie was of stout frame and temperament, but his panels were made of aluminium alloy, which was easily damaged. There was a gulley alongside him, Archie had seen these before, they fill with grubby run-off water from the road, passing motors would spray this over any unfortunate so parked. Archie had seen it happen to other older vehicles, much to his shame, he had done the same when in his primped up youth. Drive as fast as you can through any standing water, and plaster any poor old motor parked nearby, particularly if it looked like they had just been cleaned! It was a laugh, a giggle, it didn't matter, but as they say, what goes around comes around, now Archie was the old motor parked nearby, what did he expect.

Archie settled into his new home, he did get blasted with spray, which left him looking like he had been through a mud bath. But wheelman regularly washed him in an attempt to alleviate the problem, he even dried him with a chamois leather. Archie couldn't believe his luck at being leathered dry, this hadn't happened since he was young, he was loved again at last. No one crashed into him either, well apart from the crazy postman that is, and the damage so caused was minor. Archie had been nodding off, waiting outside wheelman's shelter, he was being unloaded of provisions necessary for wheelman's continued well being and comfort. Suddenly, BANG! Archie was rudely awakened, his offside mirror smashed to pieces by a demon red postman motor. Wheelman was stood at Archie's back door at the time, he shouted loudly after postman, with words Archie hadn't heard for some time. They were words which Archie had come to recognise, were used by wheelmen at times of pain or anger, this was one of those anger times. Wheelman leapt into Archie and fired up his trusty V8, banged him into first gear, floored the throttle and dropped Archie's clutch. Now Archie had permanent four wheel drive, so no wheel spin, and Archie took off like a rat out of a trap. He was soon on the bumper of postman, Archie's wheelman was flashing his headlights and sounding his horn, but to no avail. Postman continued to tear along, straight through a set of red traffic lights, closely followed by Archie! If he had eyes, Archie would have closed them, but no need, his wheelman was driving like a hooligan, Charlie Savage would have had words! Archie followed postman into the postman sorting warehouse yard. They entered at speed, both crashing over a speed hump, who was, it must be said, taken by complete surprise. Postman stopped alongside a row of identical motors, wheelman jumped out and went to talk to him. Archie correctly surmised that wheelman was angry, he was talking loudly, and pointing with his grippers at the broken mirror, then at the postman. The postman was looking contrite, and the two disappeared into the big postman shelter. Archie relaxed, his V8 was starting to cool after its sudden and unexpected burst of activity. Archie sensed the other red postman motors looking at him. Not in a menacing way you understand, they were after all kindred beings, whose consciousness was at the whim of these crazy wheelmen. What could a motor do but take it in their stride, hope their wheelman didn't send them to an early Blast Furnace.

After a short while Archie's wheelman returned, he was clutching a new mirror, and seemed a lot calmer now. As they left the postman yard, Archie could sense the postman motor, no hard feelings? If Archie and the postman motor had grippers, they would have shaken them. The drive home was far more sedate, wheelman finished unloading the provisions, all of whom had found the ride most exciting, it's not that often after all, that a vegetable gets to participate in a high speed pursuit!

Archie was pleased that wheelman was making efforts to ensure oxidation didn't get the better of him. He had been rolling around underneath with a wire brush and scraper, cleaning all the crud from Archie's chassis, followed by the application of a very effective rust preventative. However wheelman had been a bit too enthusiastic with his scraper, he had poked a hole in Archie's chassis just above the front spring hangers, and on both sides! This could be terminal, Archie was aghast, he knew wheelman could not weld, his previous repairs had been bolted and riveted in place. All was not lost, wheelman had some steel plate, he made paper templates and cut the steel to fit. Then off to see 'H', a chap of great mechanical ability and a natty welder. 'H' had Archie's offending under parts welded up in no time at all, Archie felt quite spruce. However the welding process did remind him of the Blast Furnace, memories held deep within Archie of previous consciousness, it made Archie uncomfortable in a way he couldn't quite explain.

Near 'H's workshop was a large warehouse which held a myriad of Land Rover parts, they were mainly second hand or old stock. The second hand parts had come from broken Land Rovers, those whose chassis had succumbed to the devil of Oxidation. Archie could feel the consciousness of those parts, reaching out to be part of a motor again, patiently waiting their turn to be taken from the shelf, given a purpose. These parts were lucky, some wheelmen didn't appreciate old motors, sent them to the Blast Furnace and oblivion, even though some parts had many more useful miles in them. But not these parts, Tone the warehouse gatekeeper, appreciated every single spare part in his care. He carefully, and with great skill, would fettle old engines and gearboxes back to perfect running order, ready to resume their purpose with another Land Rover, blending together to form the whole smooth running and stout hearted machine. Archie's wheelman used to take him to the warehouse quite often, buying small parts to keep him fettled. Archie liked the warehouse, he could feel the aura of all the other machines that were so like him. His wheelman brought Archie some rear springs from Tone, they were second hand one ton springs, Archie could feel the buzz of their excitement at a new beginning as they were loaded aboard. Archie could also feel the sadness in his own tired and sagging springs, they knew that their time was done, they were beyond repair. Realised that it was inevitable, in the end all motors and their parts go to the Blast Furnace.

Archie became aware some years into his custodianship with wheelman, that Tone had taken ill, then passed away, his warehouse closed. Archie was saddened, Tone was a very fine and gifted wheelman, always helpful, a thoroughly good egg. Archie thought that some wheelmen shouldn't be allowed to pass away.

After the purchase of his new old springs, Archie was driven back to his lay-by, and there at the side of the road, wheelman fitted Archie's new leaves. Archie was very pleased, he rode higher off the ground, didn't sag at the first mention of work, a Land Rover shouldn't sag, it's very embarrassing. Archie knew that sagging rear springs would cause his mud flaps to drag on the road, this is uncomfortable for the mud flaps as they abrade and wear out. Of more concern however, is that the dragging mud flaps flick innocent stones up into the path of following motors and smash their windscreens. This causes the damaged motor some angst, and leave's the innocent stone trying desperately to explain that the smashed screen is nothing to do with them. They were just patiently waiting for a passing bus to pick them up in its tyre, when FLICK! There they were, sitting in the front seat of a passing car, together with a load of smashed toughened glass, explain that if you will!

4. GOATS

Archie had settled in with his new wheelman quite well, he was comfortable now in his lay-by parking spot. He realised his days of lazing in the golf club car park were long gone, he was more likely to end up at the council tip, with a load of goat droppings to dispose of. Why was this you might ask, well, Archie had recently been taken to the depths of Suffolk. Wheelman had dipped his V8 sump and topped it up with best quality 20/50, filled his tank with some 95 Ron petroleum, (none of that ethanol green stuff), loaded up with lady wheelman and miniatures, and off they went. Wheelman was driving with gusto, giving Archie's V8 lungs a good airing, Archie was soon up to his 65 mph cruising speed, it's a good speed, faster than the lorries, slower than the rush about cars. Wheelman can relax and enjoy the view, not getting involved in the headlamp flashing duels and undertaking swoops. Archie settled into his 65 mph cruise to the east, out into the countryside away from the urban smoke. The miniatures were very excited at seeing all the cows and sheep which were out in the fields, it was a lovely sunny day. Archie and his wheelman family were in good spirits, they arrived at a farm in due course, the gatekeeper there making appreciative noises about Archie, and commenting on his quiet tick over. Before he knew it, Archie had two small goats in his cargo area, and was back up to 65 mph, headed for home. The wheelman family were all very happy at the new additions, though the two young goats were understandably just a bit scared.

Archie could understand this, as a young and inexperienced Land Rover in the Namib, he had been scared of occasion. He had quite liked a swift shot of octane booster to steady him up, but as his confidence had grown, he found he didn't need the artificial stimulant. Some of Archie's later wheelmen had, on cold mornings, given him a snifter of pure Ether straight into his air intake. Well that stuff really wakes a motor up, his V8 would start up like its sump was on fire! Archie realised early on that Ether was dangerous stuff, it felt really good, made his V8 feel like it was supercharged, without it Archie felt lethargic on start up, and this took some miles to clear. Archie even knew some diesel Land Rovers that were hooked on the stuff, used once or twice on cold mornings and they couldn't start without it, needed a top end re-build before they could kick the habit. Archie realised the danger of additives, and tried to keep clear of them.

On arrival back at wheelman's shelter, the young goats were unloaded, thereafter Archie had a regular job of transporting goat droppings and used bedding to the local tip. He did notice that his interior had a somewhat farmyard air about it after each of these jaunts, this would clear after a few miles, and wheelman would take the peg off of his smell receptor!

Archie was aware that he had an issue, it wasn't offensive in any way, just that his gearbox was noisy and sang at quite a high octave. Now, Land Rovers are not noted for their quietness, but Archie's box needed a rebuild. Tone the gatekeeper at the parts warehouse had offered a new gearbox to wheelman, the problem here though was that the box cost a lot of petrol tokens, as Tone explained, 'gears are not cheap.' Unfortunately Archie's wheelman was not flush with petrol tokens, a new box would have to wait, a roll of carpet was purchased and many layers were laid across Archie's transmission tunnel. This didn't cure his singing problem, but it did at least mean wheelman could dispense with the earplugs!

Archie had been out for a drive one afternoon, he was negotiating a small roundabout when BANG! A small Ford had tried to drive underneath him, and was now firmly wedged. Wheelman had jumped out and gone to speak with the Fords wheelman, but before anything could be done, the Ford had lurched backwards out from underneath Archie, leaving its front panel and headlamps on the road. The Ford looked very embarrassed, but what could he do, when at the mercy of a wheelman who quite plainly couldn't see the gripper in front of his face. Archie and the Ford shrugged, one day these wheelmen would learn, pay attention to what they are doing, some of them seemed to have the attention span of a goldfish. Archie was wounded though, the lower door sill and both his left hand side doors were dented, Archie could feel new parts coming along, maybe even new paint!

5. NEW PARTS

Archie languished for a few weeks with dented bodywork, he was ok to drive but he felt shabby. He was still sporting the quick blow over paint job from Spud, now plus dents. One morning wheelman arrived earlier than usual, Archie was still snoozing, he was awakened by the slamming of his drivers door. Why do they do that? Archie would ask himself, his door catches are nicely oiled, all it takes is a gentle pull and the door snicks shut. There is no need to try and make the off-side door become the near-side door, it damages the door seals, which makes Archie draftier than he is already. Wheelman fired Archie up, he had a map with him, and a flask and sandwiches, Archie suspected they were going on a trip. His suspicions were confirmed when wheelman filled him up with best quality unleaded, and they were off, M25, M1.

Archie hadn't been on the M1 since his youth, they used the motorway to check out his high speed running, 95 mph the test wheelman took him up to. That was ok back then, as

Archie had been on top form, the test wheelman didn't need nerves of steel. Not so now, his spring bushes were worn, as were his steering ball joints. Archie was still legal and safe, it's just that he had become a bit slack with age, rather more care was needed to keep him on the straight and narrow.

Archie continued on at his regulation 65 mph, two hours running and wheelman was headed for the exit, Loughborough. Archie wondered where they were going, he had noticed that wheelman had brought a Land Rover magazine at the petrol dispensary, it was open at the parts for sale page. Was wheelman going to buy some new doors, Archie hoped so, he was tired of being driven around looking like a wreck, it wasn't doing his self esteem any good at all. Wheelman drove on for a while off the motorway, then pulled into an industrial estate, he was plainly looking for something as he kept stopping and starting. Archie saw it first, 'Land Rover Spares', wheelman pulled Archie up in front of the warehouse, jumped out and disappeared inside. Archie couldn't see inside the place as it didn't have any windows, but he could sense all the spare parts, all of them anxious to be attached to a motor and gain a purpose in their existence. Archie could feel that some parts had been in the warehouse for a long time, vehicles to which some of them could be attached were getting rare. Some parts feared they would be left on the shelf, never get to be used for the sole purpose for which they were made. Archie knew their fear, he had felt the same when he had been with Spud, that he would never get a new wheelman, never have a purpose again. Archie was hopeful he might get new parts, they would join him, become part of his consciousness, maybe some of those parts stuck on the shelf would get a chance, Archie thought that would be a very fine outcome. Wheelman returned from the warehouse, he was carrying two front doors which he loaded into the back of Archie, then he disappeared back inside. After numerous return trips, Archie was loaded with two door tops, two back side doors, door runner strip, dum-dum sealer, two shock absorbers, and two new parabolic rear springs, what a haul! Archie couldn't believe it, new doors all around and parabolic rear springs, he would be a smooth rider, no more bouncing around on 1 ton Land Rover rear springs. Archie could see this being a long and happy relationship, no more second hand car dealers, he was in second heaven. The atmosphere inside Archie was electric, the spare parts knew they had a fresh start, they would become one with Archie, making him stronger and giving themselves purpose. Archie was particularly pleased, the rear doors were old stock, been on the shelf for a long time, now they would become part of him.

Archie realised that wheelman and his family, were going to have to live on bread and water for at least a month, after such a large outlay of petrol tokens for his spare parts! He would have to be on his best behaviour and not put a tyre wrong, not that Archie was a difficult customer, not at all. However being an old Land Rover, he had what lovers of old motors call 'character,' this is a polite way of saying, 'unreliable.' Archie agreed that he did indeed have 'character,' but the term irritated him. It was true that some damp mornings he was reluctant to fire up, but this was due to his dodgy coil. Shown the slightest bit of damp and it kept its sparks to itself, refused to send them down the high tension cables to his champion plugs! If wheelman were to fit a new coil he would indeed be reliable, and have 'character' all at the same time. The coil issue was a source of irritation to Archie, he had decided that of occasion, his wheelman was not the sharpest knife in the box. This was particularly so, when having failed to discover Archie's dodgy coil, he would drop Archie's bonnet to shut it. There was a very heavy 7.50 x 16 radial tyre bolted to it, the concussion of Archie's bonnet being dropped was enough to make a motors headlamps fall out!

Even the man in yellow had failed him. Whilst in the depths of Norfolk on a very damp day, said coil had decided to keep his sparks to himself. Archie simply could not start, as much as he would have liked to, it was after all very uncomfortable, sitting on that wind swept, rain battered sea front. Archie was diagnosed as needing a new starter motor, the current one was smoking. Well that was hardly surprising, the amount of work it was doing, because Archie's coil was being so selfish. Archie was distressed, his starter motor had been with him all his existence, it was a genuine Lucas article. He didn't want to lose it, after all, what sort of way is that to treat a hard working and reliable component. That coil really got up Archie's smell receptor, or it would have done if he had one. So the deal was done. Archie lost a perfectly reliable starter motor, and wheelman lost a wedge of holiday petrol tokens. On top of which, Archie was still stuck with that coil! At least Archie's starter motor would have another existence, in the consciousness of another V8 motor, following his rebuild at the auto electricians shop.

Archie made sure that his drive back home from Loughborough was a pleasure for his wheelman. Made sure his rather tired spring bushes and steering ball joints tightened up, put in a bit of extra effort. He couldn't do much to make his gearbox any quieter, but he encouraged his carburettors to be a bit more frugal with the old petroleum spirit. Save wheelman a few petrol tokens to put toward his bread and water. The ride back home went without incident, wheelman was very happy, told Archie he ran, 'as sweet as a nut.' Archie was very happy, as were his new parts. If it had been possible for spare parts to party, it would have been one heck of a shin-dig, much drinking, dancing, and laughing would have taken place. As it was, Archie and his new parts buzzed with the anticipation of refurbishment, and that word means a lot in Land Rover circles.

The day came when wheelman carefully removed all four of Archie's doors, Archie was sad to see them go, as were they to leave him. Oxidation had got the better of the steel door frames, in fact there wasn't much steel left. Archie knew that wheelman would take the old parts to the recycling centre, they would have to suffer the brief pain of the Blast Furnace, but then they would be re-born as new parts. It was with much excitement that Archie received his new doors, springs and rear shock absorber's. He was happy and felt top-notch, and he hadn't felt top-notch for quite some time. Then there was the icing on the cake. Archie knew he would need a new paint job, he was going to shine again, wheelman might even give him a waxing, he was a very happy Land Rover.

The new paint was excellent, it was still Ford Ambassador Blue, but Archie had grown to like the nice dark colour that it was. He realised he had been a bit of a snob about the paint thing, had decided to wear it as a mark of brotherhood with the now departed Ford Granada, which wheelman used to own. All said and done, they were the same under the tin, or aluminium alloy in Archie's case. 'H' had done an excellent job on Archie's paint, he shone like a new pot, and although Archie wasn't new, far from it in fact, he had that fresh out of the box feeling. Archie had even heard 'H' tell wheelman, that in a few weeks time, when the paint was good and hard, he could be washed and waxed! In the meantime wheelman was being extra careful with Archie, in car parks he would be parked away from other motors, so that thoughtless other wheelmen didn't damage his new paint. Archie realised that off roading was now out of the question, he had become too precious. Archie didn't mind though, as wheelman used him as the ultimate utility vehicle, you name it, Archie got to carry it!

6. MUD

When wheelman first took custodianship of Archie, he had taken him to an off road site. Now Archie in his youth had been to many places, and crossed all sorts of terrain, but this place was a different matter all together. The first slope that Archie came to was like stepping off a cliff, he was in low box second gear, centre diff-lock engaged. Archie didn't know why wheelman had bothered, he just shot down the slope like a sled on the Cresta Run. Archie was impressed with wheelman, his nerve had held, he hadn't touched the brake pedal. This may have been due to the fact that he had both pedal pumpers braced in Archie's bulkhead, and both grippers firmly clamped to his steering wheel. There had been a slight pause at the bottom of the slope, Archie's wheelman had got out and leant on Archie's front wing. Archie was a bit concerned, as he noticed that wheelman had one of his grippers held to his core, he was gasping air in through his front piece. Between these gasps he heard wheelman say, 'What sort of lark was that!' Now Archie definitely hadn't seen any Larks flying about, what was this new wheelman on about?

Then there was trying to get back up the slope, no chance at all. Wheelman drove with some gusto to gain enough speed for the climb, but every time Archie stopped halfway up and slid back down the slope. The only way out was through a water filled ditch, which for some reason also contained old tyres. Archie had to clamber over these, as well as making sure none of the dirty ditch water got onto his electrics, or into his trusty Stromberg's. Then there was the ice problem. On the day of the visit it was early January, ice was floating on the surface of the ditch water, as Archie entered, this very cold water entered his brake drums, and any other cavity it could find. When he finally climbed out, most of the water escaped, happy to be laying at the lowest level it could find. However a small amount remained on the surface of his brake drums and shoes, this immediately froze, Archie could feel it happen, he just hoped wheelman wouldn't need to brake any time soon. As it happened, Archie got wheelman home without incident, however Archie found that stopping in a straight line was now particularly difficult. Wheelman had to strip down his brakes, and clear all the silt out of his drums before he was back on the straight and narrow. This may have been the reason that Archie wasn't taken off road again, or was it something to do with that Lark? None of this mattered now though, Archie was revelling in the glory of his new doors and paintwork. His new parts were very happy too, they could feel the wind in their seams and hinges as Archie rushed along, Archie's self esteem was much improved, he had a twinkle in his headlamps which had been missing for some time.

Archie's life now was very different from the early days. 1976, he had been a test bed for new parts, he was important but not loved. Then he became the factory hack, used by whoever needed to get from one part of the factory to another. Archie didn't mind, it had been stressful being a test bed, hard work and quite dangerous. Testament to this was the fact that some of his twelve compatriots didn't survive, Archie was quite happy to chill and take it easy. He was after all in the place of his creation, many of his parts had been forged here from virgin steel and aluminium alloy. Archie liked the brotherhood he felt with all the newly created Land Rovers, they treated him like the knowledgeable elder that he truly was. Many sought his guidance on how they should deal with the wheelman when they finally left the plant, gained their first custodian. After four years Archie was moved to the museum, not as a display piece, his importance not recognised at this stage. He was used by the museum to move around exhibits, sometimes he would be hitched up to a trailer and taken to collect an old and ailing Land Rover, the museum wheelmen would repair the old machine and put it on display. Archie was happy here, he had good company. The old Land Rovers had seen life, they had tales to tell, as did Archie, many a quiet hour was spent swapping tales of past adventures and exploits.

Another four years had passed at the museum in this sleepy fashion, until Archie found himself on the forecourt of a franchised Land Rover dealer. He was in his prime, he had been regularly serviced washed and waxed. He commanded top money on the forecourt, with his V8 power, permanent four wheel drive and export spec ten seat deluxe interior. After a short period so displayed, a well attired wheelman handed over a large wedge of petrol tokens to take custodianship of Archie. So began Archie's first experience of life on Land Rover street.

7. UPMARKET

Archie was pleasantly surprised by his new surroundings, he didn't know much about upmarket, but that was what he had just moved to. Archie was parked alongside the stables, he had his own two horse, two axle trailer, it was all aluminium and it gleamed. The stables were quite roomy, having sufficient space for two horses, and nearby a paddock for the horses to be exercised. On the other side of the yard was a garage, which housed what Archie guessed was his new custodians hobby.

Through the half open door, Archie could see a gleaming MG Midget, light blue in colour, black soft top and silver wire wheels. There was a red and black Matchless motorcycle, and a very rare blue Raleigh moped. This new wheelman was definitely interested in motors, which Archie thought was a definite plus. To one side of the garage was a two axle vehicle trailer, Archie looked forward to runs out with either, horse or car shows who cares, it's a day out.

Archie settled into his new home and soon got to know what his duties were, and what was expected of him. A regular job was transporting the two horses to shows, Archie would have to drive particularly smoothly, or the horses would play up, kick out and damage the horse box. The Horse box trailer was an American, from the south so he told Archie, his name was Hank, and he was a laid back sort of character. Hank didn't make too much fuss when the horses kicked him, he just asked Archie to accelerate and brake, 'real smooth,' so as not to aggravate them. Archie had only seen a flash of anger once from Hank. The two horses had been playing up, pushing and shoving one another, in doing so they had been banging at Hanks sides and kicking his floor. They were on the motorway at the time, running at sixty miles an hour, Hank was towing nicely as he always did. Archie realised that Hank was getting annoyed at the horses behaviour, he felt Hank snatch at his tow hitch for no apparent reason, on a couple of occasions. Archie's wheelman hadn't noticed anything was wrong, hadn't noticed the snatch of the trailer through Archie's chassis, he was blissfully unaware of what was about to unfold. Archie was half expecting it, but even he was a little surprised when suddenly Hank started to snake, this had never happened before. Wheelman accelerated to try and calm things down, wrong move thought Archie, but it was all the excuse Hank needed. He suddenly whipped sideways, first to the left, then to the right, Archie only just managed to remain in a straight line! Hank deliberately blew a tyre with a terrific bang, then dropped back in line behind Archie, as if nothing had happened.

Archie's wheelman panicked, he could feel wheelman's grippers on his steering wheel, tighter than ever before. Then he turned Archie sharply onto the hard shoulder and stamped on the brake, Archie responded by slamming his brakes on, and quickly shuddering to a halt. Archie knew straight away that Hank had done it all on purpose, had to be the case, since Hank had stopped in a perfectly straight line behind him. Archie's suspicions were confirmed when he felt the vibrations of Hanks laughter through his tow hitch. Archie's wheelman leapt out and ran to the trailer, obviously concerned for his horses welfare. Archie assumed all was well, apart from Hanks vibrations, it was perfectly still and quiet, either that or both horses were dead, which Archie thought most unlikely.

After a while a wheelman in a yellow van turned up to change Hanks blown tyre. Wheelman, having decided that enough was enough, turned for home at the first intersection, the journey back home went smoothly. The two horses were very quiet and well behaved, but Archie thought wheelman seemed a bit dejected, once or twice he dumped Archie's clutch in an ill tempered manner, most unusual. That was no problem though, Archie had suffered far worse back in the old test bed days, and in any case, his LT95 gearbox was bullet proof.

On arrival back at the stables the two horses were unloaded by wheelman. Archie thought they had a dishevelled look about them, they were a bit unsteady on their kicking sticks, as if they had been inside a tumble dryer. Archie chatted with Hank later that evening. He told Archie that by the time wheelman had managed to stop, both horses had a look on their front pieces, that horses only have, when a wheelman is stood behind them with a hot jacket potato in his gripper! Archie and Hank did have a good laugh, more to the point though, the horses didn't misbehave again, and always treated Hank with some caution!

Archie and Hank became the best of mates, as did Archie with the car trailer, Emlyn. He had been around for a while, told Archie this was the best job he had ever had. No loading up with dirty old scrappers or accident write-offs, all he had to do was carry the MG and two bikes to auto shows, and the occasional track day. The MG was called Morris, like Archie he had started his consciousness in the black country. Morris explained to Archie that he wasn't road legal, as wheelman was into sprints and track days. Morris had been heavily modified, which was why Archie had to trailer him about on the back of Emlyn. He still had his original 1275cc engine, but this had been rebuilt and supercharged, Morris now had 150 bhp under his bonnet, which was very healthy for a car the size of a midget. His gearbox casing was original but had been rebuilt with straight cut close ratio gears, his rear axle fitted with a limited slip differential. Morris's brakes had come in for some upgrading by means of ventilated discs, oversize callipers and a brake servo. Otherwise Morris was a quiet sort of a chap, until wheelman gave him his head of course. Then he would snarl and growl and see off much bigger and younger cars. Archie loved to see Morris out cornering and leaving for dust some quite fancy cars, his supercharger whining louder and louder as he powered out of each corner.

Mike the Matchless was an interesting character, he was from the rock and roll years, the 50's, he had spent most of his consciousness on the south coast near Portsmouth. Mike had stories of burn-ups along the A27, gathering with his mates at Bert's café, the fights his handlebar man had with other handlebar men, then with the policemen who tried to sort it all out. Mike could remember one particular policeman who didn't have a motor. He would turn up on his own on his pedal pumpers, take on anyone who wanted to fight, and he almost always won. The handlebar men called this policeman the Lone Ranger, they got to like the Lone Ranger, as all the trouble makers stayed away from Bert's place when he was about.

Mike also had tales of hitting the ton along the North Circular road in London, near the Ace café. The fun they had avoiding the traffic police, black rats he called them. Then in the 60's, Mike and his handlebar man would go down to Brighton in a gang, to fight with other handlebar men, who rode funny little Italian bikes with small wheels and enclosed engines.

Mike explained that it all started to go wrong for him when the Japanese bikes arrived. They were laughed at in the beginning, but very soon Mike had been replaced by a brand new Japanese machine. None of the handlebar men wanted an old machine like him anymore, left him languishing at the back of an old garage, his paint and all his chrome work shabby and oxidising. Mike was sure he was destined for the Blast Furnace, until he was rescued by Archie's new wheelman. He was collected on Emlyn, brought back to the garage here, then wheelman set about slowly restoring him.

Mike needed quite a few spare parts as he had been badly neglected, most of which had become rare and difficult to come by. That was no problem for wheelman, he scoured the country, finding all those parts that had feared they were going to be left on the shelf. Mike said that the new old parts invigorated him, gave him a new slant on life, made him realise how lucky he was never to have felt that 'on the shelf' feeling. He was very happy with his lot, wheelman would take Mike out on classic bike runs and to classic bike shows. Mike really enjoyed these, he got to meet up with old friends and chat about their tearaway pasts. There were even a couple of restored police Triumphs, they would have a good laugh with them, reminiscing about the Ace café and all the antics they got up to.

Then there was Walter, the moped. He was pretty much a bicycle with a 50cc two stroke petrol engine attached. He had been built by the Raleigh bicycle company, he was exceedingly rare. He had been rescued from a scrap yard, stored in a garden shed for some years, before wheelman had brought him. Unfortunately there were no spare parts, all had gone to the Blast Furnace, and wheelman had to spend quite a lot of petrol tokens getting new spare parts made. Walter realised how lucky he was to exist at all, as a result he made the most of each day, didn't worry about tomorrow. Archie thought Walter had the best attitude of any restored machine he had ever met, never ever did he hear Walter complain about anything, he was just happy to exist.

As you can imagine, Archie was very happy with his lot. He had good friends, was well looked after, and didn't have to work too hard. He even had the opportunity to travel abroad, that hadn't happened since his test bed days. There was one particular trip which sprang to mind. Wheelman was taking Archie and Hank down to a horse show extravaganza in Marseilles, intending to bring back a couple of young horses. It was a great trip, Hank was empty on the way down, so he was happy, Archie didn't have to worry about any moody horses, so he was happy. They just rolled along, took in the views, chilled in the evening, and chatted rubbish like chaps do.

When they got to Marseilles, there was this tricky big junction, all the French wheelmen appeared to be in the most urgent rush. Honking their horns and shouting, cutting in and behaving like their shelters were on fire. Then they came to the traffic policeman stood in the middle of the junction, he had a whistle which he was blowing, whilst furiously waving his grippers in the air. He seemed to take a dislike to Archie, Hank and their wheelman, who had stopped to ask directions. The policeman started shouting at wheelman, in a language which Archie would describe as French. He knew it was French, because it was accompanied by a lot of gripper waving, spittle, and oh yes, they were in France! Then he started banging on Archie's bonnet with one on his grippers, this had a detrimental effect upon their wheelman, no longer calm and relaxed, he suddenly jammed on Archie's gripper brake, and leapt from Archie's driver's seat in a very animated fashion.

Archie's wheelman and the French policeman, then engaged in a discussion of the merits of driving in France. It seemed to Archie to centre mainly on the abilities of first French, and then British drivers. He could tell that it was all getting very excited, both

Archie's wheelman and the policeman were shouting loudly at one another, waving their grippers in the air. There was further banging on Archie's bonnet by the French policeman, which Archie felt was unnecessary and particularly rude. Unfortunately at this juncture, Archie's wheelman tried to knock the policeman's hat off with one of his grippers. This for some reason made the policeman even angrier, he produced some silver bracelets from his belt, which he then tried to attach to wheelman's gripper sticks. Archie could sense the aura of the bracelets, they were made of stainless steel and would never oxidise, thought they would never have to face the Blast Furnace and answer for their misdeeds. Archie could feel their aggression, intent on inflicting pain on his wheelman, he decided enough was enough. Archie released his gripper brake and rolled forward, directly onto the policeman's pedal pumper! Archie isn't an aggressive sort, but he doesn't like injustice or rudeness, and he had become quite protective of his wheelman. Now Archie weighs 1850 kilograms, which in good old English is 4000 pounds, or 1000 pounds per wheel. His footprint is roughly 25 square inches, and therefore the pressure on the policeman's pedal pumper is 40 pounds per square inch, or 1000 pounds weight, or 462 kilograms, or almost half a metric tonne. Whatever way you look at it, and whichever measure you chose to use, metric or good old imperial, that is going to hurt!

The main point here though, is that the policeman was distracted from his purpose, and dropped those nasty mean minded bracelets on the road. Archie could sense their anger at being thwarted, the policeman didn't seem too happy either. He started shouting very loudly, thumping on Archie's bonnet and front wing with both grippers, and his front piece had gone a very bright red colour. Archie recognised this as a condition which affects all wheelmen, when they are angry, or they have done something which they rather wish they hadn't. Archie thought that both circumstances had been satisfied in this instance.

Wheelman was an intelligent fellow, he knew when to take advantage of a situation, Archie saw him raise one of his gripper digits in an upward fashion toward the policeman, then stamp one of his pedal pumpers down onto the policeman's otherwise unoccupied pedal pumper. That would be the one which Archie wasn't currently parked on top of. He then jumped into Archie's drivers seat, banged him into first gear, gave Archie plenty of gas and dumped the clutch. Archie duly obliged and moved off at quite a pace.

Now Hank had missed out on all the action, since he was currently at the rear, attached to Archie's tow hitch. But he too thought that wheelman was a top egg, and didn't hold with anyone or anything, abusing said wheelman. Hank, as I have mentioned is an American, he is bigger and broader than most Brits, it's the way of things, it's how he is built. Also he is louder and can sometimes act rashly, this is not a criticism, merely an observation. Due to these fore mentioned facts, Hank is wider than Archie, just wide enough in fact to drive over, should he so chose, both of the policeman's pedal pumpers. Which is where the rashly bit comes in, Hank thought, why not, the onion eater deserves it! Archie felt the slight lurch, heard the policeman shout even more profanities, in French of course, then felt Hank laughing through the tow hitch.

Wheelman continued to drive in a very spirited fashion, whilst shouting good old English expletives out of the window. Archie was impressed at the range of wheelman's vocabulary, who patted Archie on the dashboard, whilst muttering about having forgotten to put the handbrake on! Archie smiled to himself, later that evening, he and Hank would have a good chat about the day's adventure, they made a good team.

8. CUT PRICE

Unfortunately for Archie time passed, wheelman decided to treat himself to a new Land Rover, it was a turbo diesel, so plenty of power for less petrol tokens. Archie was put in part exchange with the dealer, he was back on a garage forecourt again, with a price in his windscreen. Archie noticed that he was towards the back, and he was, putting it bluntly, cheap! Archie was thankful though, he had time to say goodbye to his friends. It was a sad parting, they were a top bunch, the good thing was that Hank and Emlyn would keep their jobs, pulled by the new Land Rover. The new boy had better have his wits about him though, both Emlyn and Hank were old hands, he was a short wheelbase, he was going to have his wheels full keeping those two on the straight and narrow.

And so Archie had loitered around at the back of the garage forecourt, it was quite peaceful back there away from the main road. All the new Land Rovers were up the front, primped and polished, they tended to ignore

Archie, thought they knew it all. They had all that new technology, turbocharged, intercooled common rail diesel power. Didn't think they could learn anything from Archie, looked down on his petrol V8. Well they and their new custodians would learn, never ignore the past, not everything that is new is good. They didn't have a locking centre differential like Archie, relied on a fancy computer controlled braking system. Then there is the turbo and intercooler, certainly not bomb proof, any problems with either of these and there is a big loss in power. Worse still the turbo blows an oil seal, then the engine can run-away, run to revolutions never intended and blow up. They couldn't be told, had to learn the hard way, simple is best, that was Archie's adage. He had lived by that, and it had served him well, at least he didn't have particulates!

Every now and again Archie's peace and quiet would be interrupted by a tyre kicker, Archie wished wheelmen wouldn't do that. It was rude to jar a being into wakefulness, they wouldn't like it if he drove onto one of their pedal pumpers now would they! Then for the most part, once mention was made of Archie's

V8 heart, they lost interest and went to look at one of the diesel Land Rovers. One day, a rural looking wheelman started looking around. Archie knew he was rural as he was wearing a flat cap, held his trousers up with both braces and belt, and wore Wellington boots which were accessorised with cow dung! This wheelman had a good look around Archie, opened the bonnet, peered at his V8, then demanded a test drive! Archie was most surprised, this hadn't happened in a while, the dealer suggested the rural wheelman look at some of the newer Land Rovers. Rural wheelman refused, said he wanted something simple, Archie definitely fitted that bill.

Once Archie's tyres were suitably inflated, off they went, at quite a pace in fact. Rural wheelman gave Archie quite a workout, then suddenly turned into a muddy field, banged in Archie's difflock, and gave it some welly. Archie was surprised, the dealer definitely was, rural wheelman tore up the field as if he owned it! On returning to the forecourt, the rural wheelman pulled out a wedge of petrol tokens, told the dealer he would take Archie provided all the mud was washed off. He then reprimanded the dealer for selling a vehicle in such a muddy condition, before marching off with the instruction that he would collect Archie the following day! Archie was pleased, the new wheelman seemed a down to earth fellow. The dealer muttered something about 'muddy field,' thrust the wedge into his pocket, and dutifully got out the pressure washer. Archie knew this was going to be different, he could feel the notion of hard work and mud coming on. That didn't matter, at last he had a new custodian.

As arranged, Archie's new wheelman arrived the following morning. He had spruced himself up a bit, removed the cow dung from his Wellingtons, and was wearing a clean pair of braces, Archie could tell that this fellow knew how to dress for an occasion! The new wheelman, quite delicately for the big ham grippered lump that he was, snicked Archie into gear, and pulled away with some finesse. Archie was impressed, this new wheelman knew a thing about driving Land Rovers.

9. THE FARM

So it came to pass that Archie arrived at his new home, 'Trafalgar House Farm,' which sounded very grand. He found himself parked up between a cattle shed, and a barn, which housed an old Massey Ferguson tractor, and a water Bowser. It all looked a bit well worn and in need of some renovation, Archie felt that the reality of the place did not live up to its name, he would have to wait and see. Archie was left parked overnight, the tractor wasn't very talkative, obviously wary of the new boy. That was fine with Archie, he had been around for long enough to understand how it all worked, like the pecking order in a hen house. In the meantime he got his head down, Archie wanted to he ready for whatever the morning brought.

Archie was still asleep when his new wheelman jumped in and slammed Archie's door. It wasn't the best of ways to be woken in the morning, he preferred to gradually slide into wakefulness. Today that wasn't to be. Archie realised this was a new start, he had better be on best behaviour, no tardy start-ups allowed, he hoped that his Stromberg's were in the wide-awake club. They most certainly were after wheelman had dragged their chokes fully closed, it's a bit like having the duvet whipped off on a cold morning! Wheelman turned the key, Archie's genuine Lucas starter motor was on the ball, having been woken by the violent slamming of Archie's drivers door. Not so Archie's V8, he was still in the land of nod, when he was hit by a fully choked petrol air mixture, which is a bit like waking up to a double scotch! Understandably Archie's V8 coughed just a few times, before settling into a nice fully choked fast idle. Archie just hoped that the new wheelman wouldn't leave his Stromberg's on full choke for too long, he knew his V8 well, it was a bit of a lightweight in the drinking department, some would say frugal! Archie's V8 couldn't take his petrol-air mixture too strong, it made him light headed and he would forget to combust properly, then he would start to splutter, the fateful words 'poor starter' would spring to mind. This wheelman was on the ball, recognised when Archie's Stromberg's needed their chokes opening, had Archie's V8 running sweet as a nut! Archie was impressed, this wheelman certainly knew his onions, or carburetted V8 motors in this case, wheelman opened Archie's chokes at the perfect moment, Archie was good to go!

Wheelman dropped Archie into gear and eased out his clutch nice and gently, Archie didn't have power steering, but that was no problem to this wheelman, he had muscles in his spit besides anywhere else. Archie was driven along a narrow track which led between fields, one of which he had been test driven in, the muddy one, which wheelman plainly did own! As the track became steeper, Archie felt his front wheels starting to scrabble for grip, wheelman eased off the power a little, popped in Archie's centre difflock and hit the gas. Archie's wheels span-up, his super-all-grip tyres bit down through the soft top surface, found some solid ground and launched Archie up the hill. Archie was enjoying this, if he could have shouted yee-haa he would have, there was no need, wheelman did, Hank would have been very impressed. Archie certainly was, how had that come out of Archie's flat capped, braces and belt wearing, Wellington booted wheelman? Archie could see some fun ahead, but he knew he was going to have to graft, this new wheelman was going to be full on, work or play. Archie was plainly a good assessor of character, wheelman kept his foot in all the way up the ever steeper hill. On reaching the top, the ground levelled out into a field where cows were grazing, they looked on with some interest as the roaring blue Land Rover reached the top of the hill. The cows were impressed, made, 'Hey this looks spectacular,' mooing noises to one another. The old grey tractor just didn't do spectacular, but Archie's roaring V8 definitely caught their attention. In one corner of the field Archie saw a twin axle low sided goods trailer, it was loaded to the gunwales with freshly cut and split logs. Archie's wheelman dropped out the difflock and headed for the trailer, spinning Archie around and reversing up to the trailers tow hitch. Before Archie had time to gather breath, wheelman had hitched up the trailer and was back in Archie's drivers seat. He knew what was coming, wheelman put him in low box, difflock in, pulled away in third gear and headed for the track they had just blasted up. As they reached the precipice, wheelman dropped Archie into second gear, Archie felt wheelman brace his pedal pumpers in his bulkhead. He tapped on the dashboard, Archie heard wheelman say, 'Do your stuff,' before firmly gripping his steering wheel.

Archie was chuffed, that's confidence for you, he hoped his super-all-grips were paying attention and working as a team. The last thing Archie needed was one of them going for glory, and trying to do it all on their own. Archie could feel that the trailer was nervous through his tow hitch, they hadn't even been introduced, just thrown together and expected to get along immediately! Well there was no time for that now, Archie started down the hill, he had tackled worse in his test bed days, the Namib had some seriously steep dunes. The difference was the trailer, he had pulled trailers before, but Archie had got to know them, to trust them. Never before had Archie been on a steep incline with a heavily loaded trailer, whom he knew nothing about. Did their over-run brakes work? Would they brake evenly or lock-up? What about their tyres, off road or on? It all made a huge difference, more importantly, what was the trailers character? Were they brash and pushy, always in a rush? Were they lazy and couldn't be bothered? Or were they diligent and competent? Archie hoped it was the third, the last thing he needed was a hooligan trying to push him ever faster down the hill, in it for the thrill. Or a lazy incompetent, who didn't know what they were doing, didn't care if the result was a wreck at the bottom of the hill!

Archie gathered pace, gravity was pulling him, trying to accelerate him at 9.8 meters per second squared. That's a big force, its why falling from height is dangerous, the tall building has no malice at all, it's the force of gravity that's going to sort you out. Archie felt the trailer pushing, his super-all-grips were working well and together, Archie could sense them communicating, each tyre gripping the loose surface as best they could, letting the others know when a little help was needed. His centre locking diff was there, completely trust-worthy, preventing his front and rear axle differentials from losing their nerve and spinning out of control. Archie's V8 revs were rising, his Stromberg's had completely shut down to an idle, his V8 using its compression to control the front and rear prop-shafts and keep Archie's speed down. All of Archie's parts were working as a team, just as he knew they would!

The trailer started to push harder, Archie's speed began to gather, he felt his rear springs lift slightly as the trailer tried to rush down the slope. His rear tyres started to scrabble for grip as the weight on them reduced, his fronts were digging in, trying to hold him back. Archie felt his rear springs lighten even further, this could be bad, it could be a roll-over! Archie felt wheelman grip his steering wheel even tighter, heard a hiss as he sucked in air through his front piece cutters. Then Archie felt it, the tension in his tow hitch as the trailer applied its brakes, slowing him, pulling his rear end down. Archie's rear tyres bit back into the track again as the weight came back down on his springs, gripping the loose surface as only super-all-grips can! They were back, every part of Archie could play their part now, they all knew what to do, Archie was back in control. Then Archie felt it through his tow hitch, the vibration of the trailer laughing, very funny thought Archie, I shall have to have a word with him. Then they were on the level, wheelman kept him in low box, dropped him into fourth gear and popped out his difflock. Archie was relieved, if his parts could have cheered they would, he could feel the buzz of excitement from his parts at a job well done! Wheelman drove Archie to the barn, he was whistling a jaunty tune through his front piece, tapping Archie's bulkhead with his pedal pumper. Archie could tell that his new wheelman was happy, which was a very good start to a new chapter in Archie's consciousness!

Later that evening, Archie was parked up alongside Mervyn, he was the trailer that Archie had pulled down from the upper field that morning. In fact Archie and Mervyn had brought six loads of logs down to the barn, before wheelman had decided to pack up for the day. Mervyn's consciousness had begun ten years earlier in Wales, (the place, not the large sea dwelling creature). He was constructed of heavy grade galvanised steel, had four independently sprung wheels, and an over-run brake that operated a hydraulic braking system. Mervyn was quality and he knew it, but he wasn't flash or brash, just confident. He did have a cheeky sense of humour though, hence the little trick he had played on Archie that morning. Mervyn, like Archie, had passed through the grippers of a good few hitchmen, experienced the sudden hitching up to an unknown tow vehicle. Put into a dangerous descent, with an incompetent or incapable motor. He had on a number of occasions, had to stress his draw bar well beyond its design capacity, to keep a wayward tow vehicle in check. Mervyn had been watching Archie as he broached the crest of the hill that morning. Seen the super-all-grips, saw the way that Archie rode on his springs, heard that sweet V8. Mervyn had judged Archie to be a quality tow vehicle, decided to have a little fun, he guessed quite rightly, that Archie could take it!

Archie and Mervyn became good friends, but Archie's new wheelman had set the standard, hard work and don't worry about the odd scratch. A regular job for Archie, was hauling Bowser up to the top fields to replenish the cow troughs. The old grey tractor, Fergy, had previously done this job, but he was an old motor now and a bit slow. He had all his ball bearings mind you, sharp as a knife, he was just a bit slow in the speed department. Fergy had been a revelation in his day, able to pull farm implements normally handled by much larger tractors. But technology moves on, Fergy's abilities had been surpassed by the newer machines. That didn't matter to Archie's new wheelman, he still loved his old Fergy, wouldn't dream of parting with him. He just needed a faster machine to get around all the water troughs for his expanding herd. That was his reason for buying Archie, permanent four wheel drive and a powerful engine at the fraction of the price of a new Land Rover, or any other four wheel drive machine for that matter. So Archie worked hard, up that hill with Bowser behind, that gave his transmission and tyres a good workout, but Archie and all his parts loved it. They would race around the top field as fast as possible, getting the water troughs filled, then hurtle back down the slope with Bowser bouncing around behind! Bowser had never before had such fun, and neither had Archie, but all the stones and mud thrown up by Archie's super-all-grips was beginning to take its toll on Archie's paintwork.

10. WORK

A job which Archie particularly liked was hitching up to the cattle trailer, and taking two or three cows to market. It was a good day out, Archie got to use the high range in his gear box, a rare occurrence on the farm as all the tracks were very steep. He could chill and enjoy the ride as they cruised along, and his V8 had a chance to clear the carbon from its combustion chambers. Once they reached the cattle market, and his cows were unloaded, Archie would be parked up amongst the other cattle trucks and trailers. They would chat and exchange stories about each others journeys. Archie really enjoyed the chance to chat with the foreign trucks. He knew some French and German from his test bed days, when he used to travel the length and breadth of Europe and beyond. It gave him a chance to polish it up, find out how things were on the other side of the channel. Then it would be back home. Sometimes wheelman would buy a new cow or bull, Archie would have to be particularly careful. The new animals could be a bit tetchy at being shuttled around, catch them at the wrong moment, they could do some serious damage to the cattle trailer. The saviour of the day was Archie's wheelman, he loved his cattle, would do his best to make the new bull/cow feel happy and comfortable.

Archie knew that the new animal would be happy when they got home, he had got to know all of the herd with his duties of taking water and feed to them. They were a lovely bunch, friendly, cheeky too. Archie had been caught out a few times, dozing in a corner of the field, one of them would sneak up and bellow as loudly as possible, it wasn't good for the nerves. Archie liked to be woken up gently, but it was all in jest, and the cow/bull would be quite pleased with itself, giving Archie a cheeky backward glance as it trotted away. At calving time the mothers would bring their newest offspring to meet Archie, his paintwork would get a good slobbering, which was the closest he got to a wash down as it so happened.

The Farm was a happy place, Archie had been welcomed into the family that it was, wheelman was a caring and hard working fellow. Archie knew that the new bull/cow would be happy, but in the meantime, whilst on route back from the market, Archie was going to be at his smoothest, he didn't want his cattle trailer getting a battering. Patrick the cattle trailer, would do his best to ensure an incident free ride back home as well. It was after all in his interest, he was the one that got a good kicking if his passenger got grumpy. Patrick was a quality cattle trailer, he towed well and never snaked, not by accident anyway. He gained his consciousness in County Armagh, Ireland. He was only a young trailer, Archie had gone over to Ireland with wheelman to collect him. He had looked splendid with his gleaming aluminium panel work, wheelman had chosen well. Patrick had three axles, was very stable, he even had a sheep deck should it be required. He made sure on the way home to smooth out the potholes, and he definitely didn't try to tease Archie by snaking. Archie could tell by the happy vibrations through his tow hitch, that all was well with the new cow/bull/Patrick. Wheelman was happy too, whistling a tune and tapping Archie's steering wheel with his grippers.

Once the bull/cow had been unloaded into the barn, wheelman parked Archie and Patrick with Fergy and Mervyn, they would all have a chat discussing their day, before settling down for the night.

One of Archie's jobs was to assist wheelman repairing the fences and gates around the farm. Mervyn worked with Archie on this job, most of the fence posts and wire he carried, but tools and off-cuts of timber were loaded into the back of Archie. For the most part, Archie's centre row of seats, were folded down to provide maximum load space. The seats themselves weren't too happy about this, being kept face down in the dark for most of the time. There was nothing Archie could do about this, it was a job, what had to be done had to be. To be honest though, the centre seats had an easy life, they just perched there enjoying the ride. Even if they couldn't see where they were going, it was an easier life than having eighteen stone of wheelman jump onto you, as did Archie's drivers seat. It wasn't the centre row seats fault of course, but the truth is, the less you do, the less you want to do. What the centre row really needed was a family, and miniature wheelmen to jump all over them, that would give them a purpose and keep them happy.

All of this physical work was taking its toll on Archie, wheelman kept him properly serviced, worn mechanical parts were replaced as and when required. Archie and Mervyn had decided that wheelman had a problem with his light receptors. There were various narrow gates which Archie and Mervyn had to be driven through, both were carrying dents and scrapes through wheelman misjudging the gap. Merv was wider than Archie, he took a short cut on bends as all trailers do, his mudguards were in a terrible state. It wasn't so much which parts were dented, as which parts weren't. Archie was sporting a serious dent to his rear off-side, numerous scrapes down both sides, and dents to both front wings. If you ever needed to picture a good hardworking no nonsense Land Rover and trailer, it was Archie and Mervyn.

Back at the barn, Archie, Mervyn, and Fergy, had been discussing the matter. Fergy had been with wheelman since he was new, arrived in 1950. Back then wheelman was a young fellow, he was still a big lump, but his ability to judge gaps was first class, Fergy had many happy undamaged years. However of recent times, wheelman had taken to ripping out gate posts. The posts were perfectly innocent, going about their business, either holding up a gate or keeping it closed, then bang! They were lying on the ground with Fergy's tyre resting on them, he would apologize profusely, putting the nod toward wheelman. Most of the time, the posts just accepted being ripped out of the ground with good grace. Wheelman after all did his best to keep the posts in good health, with regular creosoting, oiling of their latches and hinges. Some posts however gave out very angry vibrations, as if wheelman or Fergy had knocked them out of the ground on purpose. Fergy would teach them a lesson by slewing his rear tyre on top of them, he wouldn't have wheelman slated-off. All the motors and implements were after all, very fond of wheelman.

There had been problems recently on the cattle market run, wheelman's light receptor issues had caused both Archie and Patrick some concern. One occasion, wheelman had kept his foot in when a cattle truck ahead had been braking quite firmly. Archie had been relaxing, taking in the views, just cruising along. Fortunately Patrick had been paying attention, he realised that wheelman wasn't making any effort to slow down. Patrick slammed on his override brake, started snaking left and right. Archie was jerked to attention, feeling the tension in his tow hitch as Patrick tried to slow them. Archie sensed the danger straight away, could feel the presence of the cattle truck, all of his parts recognised Archie's will to stop. Archie's brake shoes slammed against their drums, immediately slowing Archie, his tyres trying their hardest not to lose adhesion on the road. Wheelman finally responded, stamping his pedal pumper on Archie's brake, taking back control of Archie. They stopped just in time. Archie nudged the back of the cattle truck, but no damage done, other than a small crease in Archie's bonnet. After that, Archie promised both himself and Patrick, that he would always pay attention. Their wheelman after all had grey fibres on his receptor holder, he needed looking after!

Archie noticed one morning, that wheelman was sporting some glazing over his light receptors. They were held up by a titanium framework, which rested upon wheelman's noise and smell receptors. Archie had seen these things before on wheelmen, they generally stopped them from bumping into things, Archie was hopeful for the sake of his bodywork. Merv had given Archie a nudge through his tow hitch when he saw wheelman's glazing, Archie could feel the vibration of Merv sniggering. He had to agree, wheelman didn't have the same air of invincibility about him, he had a sort of confused look. This didn't matter at all, most importantly, wheelman didn't hit anymore gate posts! Archie could sense they were no longer trying to make themselves as slim as possible, as wheelman roared through. Certainly if the gate posts had light receptors, they would no longer be holding them tightly shut.

Around the farm there was a more relaxed air. Wheelman was driving a lot faster now, Archie was enjoying being driven at top speed up some steep slopes, through tiny gaps without hitting anything! More to the point, the very structure of everything at the farm was no longer in fear of being damaged or destroyed. There were two exceptions to the rule though, Merv and Patrick, these trailers were wider than Archie, their bodywork sat down between the wheels. Their mudguards were very susceptible to damage, Archie could feel both trailers tense up through his tow hitch as he roared through tight gaps, he told them not to worry. Wheelman now had the light receptor sight of a sniper, and was driving as if he had a steering wheel in his grippers when his consciousness began!

Fergy was particularly happy, he no longer had to deal with bad tempered gate posts, which, courtesy of wheelman's poor light receptor sight, had just been ripped out of the ground. Some of the gate posts were just nasty though, wouldn't forgive and forget, they would vibrate their fences at Fergy as he passed. He got to know the nasty ones. Sometimes when it was slippery, he would let his rear tyres slide sideways and clump those posts as he passed. This would cause wheelman some confusion, he would stop and remove his glazing, rub a small piece of white linen over them with his grippers, before replacing the glazing and driving off. The piece of white linen he put through a hole into his pedal pumper stick covers, that appeared to be its regular storage point. It was all quite a palaver, sometimes Fergy would clump some of the nasty gate posts, just to see wheelman go through this ceremony!

11. BREAKER'S

Archie's path was about to take another turn. He had seen a new Land Rover parked up outside wheelman's shelter, a sharp looking young wheelman speaking to Archie's wheelman. The sharp looking fellow was adorned with much yellow non-ferrous metal, which Archie had come to realise was much sought after by all wheelmen. The sharp looking wheelman had walked over to Archie, given him a good looking over, kicked his tyres and sucked air in through his front piece cutters. Archie was annoyed, why kick him, it was uncomfortable and disrespectful to a being. Archie decided that given an opportunity, he was going to slip his gripper brake, roll forward and onto the fellows shiny black pedal pumper covers! Archie was an easy going being, it was just that some wheelmen, particularly this one, deserved a flat pedal pumper. It would, Archie thought, deter him from kicking innocent and half asleep Land Rovers like himself. The sharp looking wheelman then left, taking the new

Land Rover with him. Archie knew the game was up when his wheelman walked over and patted him on the bonnet, he had never done that before, Archie realised it was goodbye.

That evening Archie spoke to Merv, Patrick, Fergy, Bowser, and all the other Farm implements to wish them well. Archie had made good friends with them all, parting was sad, but Archie knew that wheelmen are only custodians for a short time. They are always tempted by the lure of newer shinier motors. Archie hoped a new wheelman would become his custodian, maybe one that wouldn't put so many dents in his bodywork. Archie also realised that although mechanically he was in fine fettle, he was no longer a pretty sight. Archie's biggest fear was that he wouldn't get a new custodian, would be broken, pulled to pieces part by part, until he was no longer one being. The parts would be put onto shelves, waiting, hoping, one day to become part of another motor, and blend with that consciousness. This fate was worse than going to the Blast Furnace, at least there he and all his parts would lose their consciousness as one.

The sharply dressed wheelman delivered the new Land Rover to the farm the following day, the new motor, cocky and full of itself, was parked up alongside Archie on his arrival. Not much passed between the two at first, but Archie could sense the new Land Rover taking in its surroundings, looking at the trailers, implements, and Archie, more to the point looking at Archie's dents! He introduced himself to the new Land Rover, who said that his name was Nigel, the cockiness was gone, Archie guessed why. He explained to Nigel that he was going to be worked hard, wheelman was a good fellow and would keep up with Nigel's servicing, but this farm was no holiday camp. Nigel asked Archie about his dents, he was concerned and feared for his paintwork. Archie explained that wheelman was a full-on worker, but a little reckless, sometimes even careless, hence the dents. Archie tried to re-assure Nigel, told him that wheelman had recently been fitted with new glazing, since then the amount of damage had decreased. Nigel didn't seem convinced, Archie could tell he thought he had drawn the short straw, no easy urban life here. Matters weren't helped when Merv and Patrick introduced themselves. Both these trailers sported serious damage to their mudguards, they gave Archie a look. Nigel was in for a hard time, they blamed Nigel for Archie's departure, being a new boy with no experience was not going to help either, Nigel would have to learn fast!

Having delivered the new Land Rover, the sharply dressed fellow assured Archie's wheelman, that Archie would be renovated, and found a new custodian. Reassured by this, Archie's wheelman gave Archie a final pat on the bonnet, and bade him farewell. The sharp wheelman drove Archie from the farm, it was a short drive, just a few miles to a lay-by, where Archie was loaded onto a recovery truck. Sharp wheelman was given a small wedge of petrol tokens by the recovery truck wheelman, after which he climbed into another new Land Rover which was waiting nearby, and left. Archie's recovery truck set off, they drove for about an hour before turning into an industrial estate, then into a salvage yard. Archie didn't think he had ever before felt so low. He was very fond of his parts, even the dented ones, they had been together for a long time, Archie didn't want to lose any of them.

Archie was unloaded and parked beside an old Bedford lorry, he recognised the model, an 'S' type. Its front axle was missing, its chassis stood on wooden blocks. Archie tried to make contact, the lorry remained silent, he let his consciousness probe the old motor, managed to rouse the Bedford, who introduced himself. His name was Yogi, named after an old cartoon character, he had seen better times, but was no longer in the best of health. This was mainly due to the fact that he had lost many of his parts, the most notable being his front axle. Yogi said that he was quite rare, which struck a worrying chord with Archie, most of Yogi's compatriots having long since gone to the Blast Furnace. He survived because some wheelmen collected and restored old motors, unfortunately for Yogi, he was being stripped to restore other 'S' types.

In his day, Yogi and others like him, had been the mainstay of the British haulage industry. Two axle rigid flat back lorries, rated at ten tons, but most often loaded to fifteen, on one occasion Yogi had been loaded to eighteen tons, that had been a struggle. He still had his engine, it was a five litre in-line six cylinder four stroke diesel, he had a four speed gearbox and two speed back axle. One of his wheelmen, many years previous, had fitted him with a radio. He never had a heater, the wheelmen relied on the heat from his engine, which was in the cab alongside them, to keep warm. Archie chatted to this old fellow for a while, found out the pros and cons of the yard. He decided there were more cons than pros. It would appear that most motors came in whole, and left as parts. Some were even subjected to the torture of the oxy-acetylene cutter, slowly dismembered by the searing point of flame. That was worse than the Blast Furnace, at least there the pain was all encompassing, then along with consciousness, it was suddenly gone. Almost merciful, all of the motors parts as one in the hot molten soup.

Archie sat in the yard for some weeks, mostly ignored by the wreaking tool wheelmen. The Old Bedford was gradually getting smaller as his parts were removed, then, one day, salvation! His cab and chassis was collected by a wheelman who was going to restore him, Yogi had been ecstatic, saved from the cutter, he couldn't believe his luck. His purchaser was a wheelman called Bill, once owned a fleet of Bedford's, made his money hauling Clementine's from the docks on the south coast, to the London Markets. Bill had sold up many years ago, now he wanted to restore an old wagon in the colours of his own from way back. Yogi was chuffed, never been happier he told Archie, this gave Archie hope, maybe he would survive the yard, only time would tell.

Archie sat there in the breakers yard, it was not a nice place to be, so many motors being taken apart, some were ripped apart by huge machines driven by the breakers wheelmen. Turned upside down and shaken so violently, that their internal combustion heart and transmission would fall out of them, crashing to the ground. He could sense the pain and fear in the motors, once the shining joy of some wheelman, now reduced to tortured pieces of ferrous and non ferrous parts. Archie hoped a wheelman would rescue him, before he too had his V8 soul shaken violently from him.

Archie was hidden away in one corner of the breakers yard, trying to be invisible. One sunny afternoon he was dozing, half asleep, Yogi had gone the previous week, replaced by a big old Leyland Octopus. This, thankfully, was hiding Archie from view. Then he felt it, that kick, he had felt the kick a number of times in his consciousness, it used to irritate him greatly, but now it brought hope. The wheelman walked around Archie, checking out his dents, then he asked the breakers wheelman to start Archie's engine. This required the use of a booster pack, as Archie's battery was in decline through lack of volts from his alternator. After a little coaxing, and some surprisingly gentle words of encouragement from the breakers wheelman, Archie's V8 coughed and then roared into life. The wheel kicker made admiring noises, he liked Archie's V8, which Archie had to admit, sounded as sweet as ever. Then he jumped into the drivers seat, checked that Archie's clutch wasn't seized, and made sure all his gears could be selected. Next thing he was underneath, banging and prodding at Archie's chassis, then he was gone, as was the breakers wheelman. Archie was disappointed, his hopes of rescue had been raised, now he just settled down to wait, trying to make himself as inconspicuous as possible. He was woken early next morning, aware of a wrecking machine making its way toward him, moving motors out of its way, clearing a path. Archie prepared himself for the turn upside down, the violent shake. Then he saw him, the tyre kicker from the previous morning, and he had a car transporter with him! Before he knew it, Archie was winched onto the back of the transporter, an old Bedford TK, Archie's hopes were raised. TK's were quite rare, this one had shiny paintwork, was the tyre kicker an admirer of older motors?

12. SALVATION

Archie was on the car transporter for a couple of peaceful hours, he relaxed, more relieved than could ever be explained. The Bedford sang along, Archie could feel the steady beat of its five and a half litre straight six diesel. Felt the smooth gear changes made by the wheelman, a four speed synchro box, the quick snap down change of the Eaton two speed axle, more leisurely on the up shift.

Archie knew exactly how the old 'S' type Bedford had felt, rescued from what Archie had thought was imminent destruction. Archie wondered too about the wrecker wheelman, the gentle words that morning for his V8 to fire up. In his moment of desperation Archie had felt the wheelmans soul, his inner being, so often hidden from view behind the hard exterior. Archie was surprised, he had never noticed that before, didn't realise wheelman had such thing.

Then they arrived, it was a small yard behind a workshop, there were old motors in various states of repair, renovation, the word that all old motors long to hear. Archie could see Oxygen and Acetylene bottles in the corner, for a moment the fear returned, then he saw the welding torch hooked up to it, and the fear subsided. The wheelman gently winched Archie down off the TK, Archie was relieved he didn't try to drive him off. Archie's brakes had seized whilst sitting in the breakers yard, they would need stripping down before Archie could stop safely. He was gently pushed into the workshop, heard the wheelman tell another that Archie just needed a little fettling and he would be good to go!

Archie had a peaceful night in the workshop, he liked the smells of the oil and grease, the tools lining the walls, toolboxes below. The trolley jacks and axle stands, all ready, waiting to get to work. Then Archie realised, they were all waiting to get to work on him, take his consciousness forward to a new chapter. He thought about his friends back at Trafalgar House Farm, of the fun they had together, all the hard work. Archie missed them, the same as he missed Hank. It was a shame when a motor moved on, that part of their existence ends forever, like a heavy and stout door closing with a loud click. That is how it is, motors must get used to it, sometimes a motor will bump into an old friend, but that is a rare occurrence.

The following morning Archie was jacked up and put on axle stands, wheelmen started pulling his wheels and brake drums off. New brake shoes and cylinder seals were fitted, drums cleaned up and replaced. Brake system bled and shoes adjusted, air and oil filter changed, fresh oil in his engine, gearbox, transfer case, axles and steering swivels, cooling system flushed and refilled. Then fresh petrol was put in his tank, a new battery fitted and his V8 fired up. Archie's V8 coughed once or twice, then roared into life. It felt good, all those new fluids, Archie felt like a new motor fresh off the production line! No more fears of the Blast Furnace or the oxy/acetylene cutter, Archie could see a new consciousness ahead, he just needed his dents sorting out.

None of that just for now though, Archie was reversed out into the yard and a pressure washer turned onto his body work. Archie didn't think the pressure washer was such a good idea, he tended to leak, had done from new, it was a Land Rover design feature. Or at least that's what Archie would tell himself, particularly when any wheelman leapt aboard Archie, without first checking his seat was dry. They learnt quite quickly these wheelmen, Archie had noticed that a bit of discomfort generally speeded the process up! As it happened, Archie enjoyed his pressure wash, his underpinnings had been given a blast as well, knocking off all that accumulated farm mud. The two wheelmen then jumped into Archie, and drove him off through the gate, slowly at first, checking that all his parts were working properly. Needless to say, all of Archie's parts were fully awake and on the job, they had after all just been pressure washed, you wouldn't be sleeping through one of those would you! More to the point, all of Archie's parts, although worked hard, were of good quality, and had, where appropriate, been kept fully greased. As a result, all of his parts had the right mental attitude, a 'can do' approach, no slackers here. Most importantly though, they liked being part of Archie, there was nothing mean or unpleasant about Archie, he was a thoroughly good egg. His aura was a happy one, his parts liked to be part of that, a good and happy team. Archie's new wheelmen were impressed. He steered in a straight line, didn't keep trying to wander off and check out the vegetation, this being yet another Land Rover design feature. He rode nicely, which was courtesy of his previous wheelman soaking his springs in oil. He stopped well, but then the new wheelmen knew he would, since they had just rebuilt his braking system. These new wheelmen knew their stuff, they had saved many an old motor from the Blast Furnace. Now they wanted to check out Archie's V8, was it up to the mark, or did it need a rebuild? They gradually explored his V8's potential, he had after all been laid up for a while, needed a little time for the fresh 20/50 to find its way into all the furthest oil galleries and journals.

Archie's V8 felt good, he had been around for some time and covered many miles, he liked all of his parts, they had been with him from the first, the last thing he wanted was to be stripped down and lose any of them. They all worked together in a well honed oily manner, he just wouldn't be the same V8 without them. Needless to say, Archie's V8 pulled it off, the wheelmen were very happy. Archie heard words such as, 'sweet as a nut,' and, 'pulls like a train.' Archie knew his V8 was in the clear when he heard the immortal words, 'give it some stick then.' It was like music to his ears, or would have been if he had any!

The wheelman dropped Archie from fourth to third gear, then squeezed his throttle fully open. At the time Archie was trundling along at 40mph, his V8 was at the perfect point on his torque curve. He responded admirably, before they knew it, Archie had hit 75mph, the wheelman up shifted Archie into fourth and hit the gas again. Archie was impressed, this was like his test bed days, these wheelmen knew how to drive a motor.

Archie's V8 was enjoying the massive amounts of petrol air mixture being drawn into his lungs, he breathed deeply and burnt the mixture perfectly in his combustion chambers. He was singing the song that only a cross plane crank V8 can sing. All of Archie's parts were working as a team, every single one giving their best, they realised that their survival depended upon a flawless performance. They delivered, Archie was flying, 80, 85, 90, 100mph. The wheelmen were laughing as Archie peaked at 105mph, they eased off, Archie dropped back to 40mph, which now seemed very pedestrian. The wheelmen were laughing and slapping their grippers together, Archie heard the words, 'what a machine,' and, 'she can fly.' Archie always thought it strange that wheelmen referred to him as 'she,' when quite plainly he was a 'he.' But that didn't matter, Archie and all his parts knew that they were safe. They would be staying together as one, Archie wondered if a new paint job was on the cards?

The wheelmen drove back to the workshop in a more relaxed manner, Archie was taking in the views. The rest of his parts were chilling too, they knew they had put on an outstanding performance. On arrival, Archie was parked up in a corner of the yard, in front of him was a car recovery trailer. He saw that it had a three ton winch, three axles, and a wide load bed sat down between the tyres. Its chassis was heavy duty galvanized steel. The trailer sensed Archie scanning him, and introduced himself, his name was Peter Reginald Gordon, though he liked to be known as Gordy. He explained that he was to be Archie's trailer, they were going to be a team. Archie was concerned that he was replacing another motor, Gordy told him not to worry. The wheelmen who had given Archie the once over, had an expanding vehicle repair and renovation business. They now had more work than Trevor the TK could deal with, so Gordy had been brought a few weeks earlier. He knew the wheelmen were looking for another tow vehicle, saw Archie brought in on the back of Trev. He had been a bit concerned as Archie looked to be in a sorry state, then he heard Archie's V8, and knew he was on to a winner.

Gordy told Archie about himself, he was a new boy, only gained his consciousness a few months ago in Cheshire. They had a good old chat, Gordy was as keen as mustard, itching to get stuck in. Archie took a liking to Gordy, he seemed an honest no nonsense trailer. Archie could see he had been well put together, with quality galvanizing and steel. He reminded Archie of three previous old friends of his, Hank, Merv and Patrick. Those three trailers had been quality, towed and stopped well, they had good times together. Trevor had woken up by now, he joined in the conversation. He gained his consciousness in 1960 in Dunstable, had worked down on the south coast for many years, general haulage, running market produce up to London and the midlands. This was before containerization, the goods were craned off the ships onto the dockside. The stevedores and Trevor's wheelman would use their grippers to load him, then wheelman would rope and sheet down the load. It was a slow process, but Trevor's wheelman had the roping and sheeting down to a fine art, and made a very tidy job. The only Motorway at the time was the M1, the A3, which Trevor regularly travelled, was winding and hilly. For this reason he had been specified with an Eaton two speed rear axle, this helped with his journey times, made him a flyer. When empty he could hit 70mph! Trevor explained that he was a luxury truck in his time, quiet with comfortable seats and a heater. Some wheelmen even used the shelf behind the seats as a bunk. The problem was that wheelmen were getting bigger, they didn't fit in Trevor's cab, there wasn't enough headroom and wheelmen got TK stoop. None the less, Trevor had been driven by many a proud wheelman, before he and his type were replaced by bigger more powerful lorries. There was one last hurrah though, lorries like Trevor were fitted with a V6 supercharged two stroke diesel engine. This truck, called a KM, was a real flyer, but just a bit noisy, and the cab was still too small! Trevor passed through the grippers of various custodians, his condition gradually deteriorating. He couldn't believe his luck when the two wheelmen here had purchased him. They put him up on axle stands, replaced all his worn out parts, converted him to a car transporter and recovery truck, finishing the job off with a fresh coat of dark blue gloss paint, excellent! Archie had to admit that Trevor looked very smart, he knew by experience that Trevor drove and pulled very well. He was wondering about his own paint job when one of the wheelmen turned up, drove him into the workshop and started knocking out his dents. Things were definitely looking up!

Archie knew from recent experience, that gaining a dent is uncomfortable, the positive ions, and negative electrons, are forced to move and realign as the metal is deformed. They are unhappy about this, they were comfortable where they were, and convey their distress to Archie. He feels the internal tearing, it reminds him of when he gained his consciousness as his parts were forged and pressed into shape. It was a violent and disturbing experience, caused him to have flashbacks of previous consciousness, before Archie ever existed. He found this unsettling, he knows he has lots of dents to fix. It is the equivalent of a wheelman having his front piece cutters removed, all of them! Archie knew it was for the best, he braced both his panels and himself for the ordeal.

The work on Archie's bodywork continued at quite a pace. The wheelmen would carefully heat each dent, start to hammer it out, then heat the area again, to anneal it, before further hammering. Each area work hardening, in danger of fracturing as its shape was changed. Archie could feel the structure of his panels being forced to change shape, some of these dents Archie had carried for many years. They had come to be part of the panel in which they were indented, the panel felt comfortable with the dents and didn't wish to lose them. They became distressed at losing their dents, it was like losing a troublesome, yet reformed family member. This distress was felt by Archie, he knew it was for the best, tried to reassure his panels, but they were stubborn and resisted. Hence the wheelmen had to apply heat, to try and relax the panels inner structure before each reshaping.

After the dents had been removed, filler was applied. This was rubbed down first with 80 grit abrasive paper, followed by a little more filler here and there. Final shaping with 80 grit, then 240 and 400 grit for a smooth finish. This rubbing down was also uncomfortable for Archie, though his panels didn't complain so much. They quite liked their dent free contour. This rubbing down was a similar feeling to Archie, so I believe, as a lady wheelman having her pedal pumper sticks waxed. Now as the writer of Archie's memoirs, this is a wild guess, I could be wrong. Better check with your own lady wheelman, Archie assures me that she will concur!

Once Archie's panel repairs were complete, he was flatted down with 400grit and water. Every part of him that didn't need paint, was covered with masking tape, and best quality newspaper. Archie was then blasted with etch primer. He needed etch primer because his Aluminium alloy panels were very rebellious. They would shed any paint that didn't have a very firm grip, the etch primer got that grip. The panels complained to Archie yet again, he was beginning to find them just a bit tiresome, like miniature wheelmen on a long road trip! Archie and his panels had been together a long time, just sometimes though, he wished they were made of sterner stuff, like steel. A less troublesome material, unless of course oxidation got to it, then the steel would start to vanish bit by bit. Wouldn't even say good bye, or think to mention it was off on a permanent holiday! No, Archie would stick with his moaning Aluminium alloy, at least it wouldn't try to sneak off. Archie was then blasted with navy blue, a very fine colour. Once the masking was removed and his tyres blacked, he was rolled out into the yard, Archie looked top notch.

Gordy would have given Archie a wolf whistle, in a slap your upper pedal pumper stick, wheelmanly sort of way. This would have been attached to a gruff and hearty voice, if he had a hearty voice, or whistle that is, which obviously he doesn't. But nonetheless, he still communicated the sentiment! Archie and all his parts were very happy, and likewise, he would have given Gordy the thumbs up, but ditto the thumbs! The move from the breakers yard to this, renovation of all things, was beyond luck. Parts of Archie could have been waiting on a shelf for dispatch to a new vehicle. Other parts could have been in a heap, waiting for dispatch to the Blast Furnace, which is an altogether different sort of dispatch. One which every part and motor, tries to avoid with the utmost diligence.

Archie was hitched up to Gordy, Trevor had already left the yard. They heard Trevor's diesel, its revs rising and falling as the wheelman worked his way up through the gears. Not so many changes though, Trevor was empty, wheelman didn't need the Eaton two-speed to help him on his way. After a short while one of the wheelman climbed aboard Archie, fired up his V8, and he and Gordy headed for the gate. The wheelman set off at a fair pace, Archie was pleased with the way Gordy towed, nicely in line with no skipping about or snaking. He could feel Gordy pushing through his tow hitch as he slowed, then felt Gordy's overrun brake operate. Archie was confident Gordy would pull well when loaded. Gordy was more than happy, Archie pulled strongly, and was heavy enough not to be pushed around on the downhill and bendy bits, keep it all under control.

The wheelman was very happy, he and his fellow wheelman had put a lot of effort into getting Archie roadworthy again, they had taken a risk, purchasing a beaten up old Land Rover from a breakers yard. They had put their trust in themselves and in Archie, now it was paying off. Wheelman was opening up those twin Stromberg throttles, and Archie's V8 was singing its song! They drove on for a while before wheelman turned Archie and Gordy into a transport café car park. He spun Archie around, and reversed Gordy up to an old black 103E Ford Popular, which was tucked away in one corner. Wheelman then disappeared into the café. Archie had noticed that wheelmen did like to pull off of the road of occasion. They would park their motors in a group, then disappear into what, quite often, appeared to be a very ramshackle shelter. Then, after a period of time, they would return, but with a satisfied air about them. In addition to which their mind would not be on the job, there was a sleepiness about them which tended to precede a dent! However, after a relatively short time, wheelman returned. Contrary to what Archie had expected, wheelman had a sort of bounce about him, almost a skip, which for a greasy wheelman was most unexpected. In addition to which he kept saying the word, 'bargain,' and, '£60,' with, 'can't believe it,' thrown in.

13. POP

Wheelman wound out Gordy's winch and hooked it to the front of the old Ford. Gordy had been dozing at the time, he was most surprised the way wheelman was dashing about, behaving a bit like a miniature at Christmas. The old Ford groaned as he was gradually hauled aboard, he had been stood for a long while. His leaf springs had started to oxidise together, his gripper brake wouldn't release, and his tyres were only partially inflated. In fact the old Ford had become accustomed to his life tucked in one corner of the café car park. He had been 'retired,' some years ago, but unfortunately oxidation had taken a hold, there was now considerably less of him than there had been! Quite large amounts had just vanished, escaped the Blast Furnace, in fact the old Ford had become quite used to the idea that he was going to quietly disappear. This though was delusion, old motors never fully escape, there are always some bits left over, the main parts, the soul of a motor, these get scooped up and into the Blast Furnace they go!

Gordy's winch was having quite a hard time dragging the reluctant old Ford onto his back, it was moaning and groaning, generally being very stubborn. Archie and Gordy were very surprised, anyone would think they were scrappers, not renovators. In the meantime, wheelman had disappeared underneath the old Ford, hammering at its brake drums trying to get them to release. Archie started to scan the old Ford, trying to find its consciousness, this was difficult, the old motor was being singularly uncooperative. Wheelman made the breakthrough, the old Ford had rod operated brakes front and rear, with a very clever compensator to allow for steering. Wheelman took a set of bolt croppers out of Gordy's tool box, then disappeared back underneath the old motor. No sooner had he made his intentions clear, than the old Ford suddenly released its brakes, and rolled with relative ease onto Gordy.

Archie heard the quiet old voice in his consciousness, 'done for now,' it said, 'almost made it,' 'now for the big heat.' Archie realised the problem straight away, let the word 'renovation,' filter through, Gordy felt the old motor go lighter on its springs, like a weight had been lifted. At last the old Ford started to listen. As wheelman strapped the old motor down, Archie explained that he had been rescued from a breakers yard by these very wheelmen. They had fixed his oily parts, knocked out his dents, and given him a splendid coat of paint. The old Ford couldn't believe his luck, his old 1172cc flathead four pot, was going to breathe petrol air mixture again, that hadn't happened in many a year! He apologised to Gordy for making his winch work so hard, told them that his name was Pop. Wheelman went back into the café, Archie knew from experience that it could be a long wait, this didn't matter though, it never did, time is irrelevant to motors. It would normally give Archie a chance for a snooze, today it gave Pop a chance to tell Archie, and Gordy, about himself.

Pop gained his consciousness in 1954 in Essex, at the Dagenham factory, he had passed through the grippers of a number of custodians, before being retired in the café car park. His first custodian was the Hampshire Police, he had been a 'Q' car, which Pop thought sounded very dramatic. Particularly since most of the time he was used as a hack, for the local CID policemen to get around in. One occasion, whilst very much the new boy, he had been parked in the back yard at Cosham police station. He had been watching the comings and goings of the big black Wolseley R/T cars, rushing out of the yard on emergency calls. It was late in the evening, the night duty CID had left Pops keys in his ignition. He was aware that something was going on, as the R/T car had just raced out of the yard, blue light flashing and bell ringing. Pop saw that it was headed south, toward Hillsley Bridge, the only way off of Portsea Island at the time. Suddenly Pops driver's door was opened, a wheelman wearing police uniform jumped into his driver's seat. Pop was most surprised, his wheelmen were always in their florals, never uniform. What would be the point, the uniform gave away the fact that he was a police motor, he would no longer be incognito!

Before he knew it, the uniformed wheelman had fired up his 1172cc flathead, dropped him in first gear, floored the gas and roared out of the yard! Pop wasn't used to this,

his flathead felt a bit heady, all that rich petrol air mixture suddenly rushing into his four pot lungs. Then the wheelman suddenly came to a stop, and waited. They were parked up by the old A3, just before it joined the Southampton Road. Pop saw the headlights first, heading north out of the city, it flashed by, a grey Mk 1 Ford Consul, there were two wheelmen in the front. The uniformed wheelman floored the throttle, and dropped Pops clutch. Pop took off like a rat out of a trap, his tyres even laid some rubber, not an easy thing to do with only 30bhp on tap! The Consul turned left at the A27, towards Gosport and Southampton, Pop followed, with his demon wheelman squeezing every last bit of power out of his very surprised 1172cc's. With 47bhp from its 1500cc motor, the Consul was pulling away on the straight bits, but Pop only weighed 700kg, and the demon wheelman hardly used Pops brakes at all. Somehow he managed incredible angles of lean in the curves and roundabouts without Pop falling over, to Pops surprise he was keeping up with the Consul! He was helped on his way by the demons encouragement of, 'well done fella,' every time they emerged from a corner upright, or managed to avoid entering a shop front. This manic driving continued until the consuls wheelman decided to park it in an ornamental pond, having completely misjudged his braking. At this point the demon wheelman leapt from Pop, and applied bracelets to the two Consul wheelmen's gripper sticks! After a short while the Wolseley's turned up, the uniformed wheelmen leapt forward to help Pops demon, there was much happiness and punching of cores with grippers. Pop heard the words, 'well done lone ranger', now he knew the demons name. The Consul was looking very embarrassed at being caught, Pop enjoyed the moment, he was regarded as old fashioned, outdated. These new Consuls could get above themselves, thought they were something special, with MacPherson strut independent front suspension, overhead valve engine, column change gearbox, they didn't even have a chassis! No wonder he ended up in the ornamental pond.

The demon then drove Pop back to the station. He was plainly very happy, kept tapping Pops steering wheel with his grippers,

Pop heard the words, 'you did well,' numerous times. Pop had to admit that he had! This drive was far more sedate, Pop was quite pleased, he wasn't used to all the high speed stuff, he had feared an early visit to the Blast Furnace at more than one corner!

After a few years with the Police, Pop was auctioned off, he was sold for a good wedge of petrol tokens, as he had a no expense spared service history. He then had a quiet suburban life, ferrying families of wheelman about, the occasional picnic and holiday. As Pop had become older, he had changed custodians a number of times, and for fewer petrol tokens on each occasion. Next the dreaded Oxidation began to take a hold on both his bodywork and chassis, his custodian at the time was the café owner. Then Pop failed the nemesis of all old motors, the dreaded MOT. The café owner decided to retire pop, he didn't want to part with him, or send him to the breakers. So Pop was parked up in the corner of the café car park where Archie and Gordy had found him.

14. SMOKEY

The Journey back to the yard and workshop went well, Pop weighed less than one ton, Gordy towed very nicely, and Archie's V8 was on song. Wheelman was also very happy, having acquired yet another old motor to restore, namely Pop. On Archie's scale of happiness, it was how he felt after an oil and filter change, followed by a wash, chamois, and a good waxing. Or, in wheelman measures, it was how wheelman felt at a particular time of the year when it was cold, they put up lots of coloured lights, and erected large pieces of vegetation inside their shelters. Archie had noticed that some wheelmen could become very happy after they had poured liquid which contained Ethanol, into the hole in their receptor holder front piece. However this did cause on occasion, wheelmen to hit one another with their grippers, fall off of their pedal pumper sticks, and then sleep in some very inappropriate places. Today though, wheelman hadn't touched a drop of Ethanol, and on arrival back at the yard, made a very tidy job of reversing Gordy up to the Workshop. Gordy's winch was run out, through a pulley at the far end of the workshop, then back onto Pops chassis. Archie's gripper brake was firmly applied, and Pop was winched off, fortunately It wasn't as difficult as getting Pop on board. He was still very stiff after being stood for so many years, but Pop knew he was on the way to renovation, not oblivion, two completely different outcomes!

Archie and Gordy were parked up in the yard, the wheelman had started to work on Pop straight away, Pop was up on axle stands, his wheels having been removed whilst he was carefully inspected. Trevor the TK then arrived, he had another old Ford strapped to his back, this was bigger, it was a Trader 75 tractor unit, with a Scammell automatic coupling. Archie could see that the old motor needed a fair amount of work, and currently was looking very sorry for itself. Archie wondered if Trevor had mentioned the word renovation, that always cheered up an old motor. The Trader was winched down from Trevor, parked alongside Archie, who could sense immediately that the Trader had a relieved air about him, as did his parts. They obviously hoped to remain as one. The trader felt Archie scrutinizing him, and introduced himself, his name was Smokey. He explained that in his early days, this had related to his ability to tear along at a fair rate of knots, which was due to his 5.4 litre straight six diesel, five speed gear box, and two speed rear axle. Later the name was more appropriate as his tired engine had a tendency to smoke, but not any more. Whilst pulling a heavy load of scrap steel up the heads of the valley road in South Wales, a piston had let go, burnt out down one side. He explained in his defence, that the heads of the valley is a long and unrelenting climb, his four in line tipping trailer had been well overloaded, grossing twenty five tons. Smokey wasn't surprised his engine had let go, the piston had been complaining for some time, his injector was faulty causing a hot spot. This didn't matter on short bursts of maximum power, but the heads of the valley wasn't a short burst.

Since then, Smokey had been out of action. His wheelman at the time of the blow up had ordered a new lorry to replace him, but he couldn't bring himself to get rid of the Trader. There had been many good times together, so Smokey was retired to one corner of the haulage yard. He was often visited by his wheelman's miniatures, they would climb up into his cab, pretend to be racing down the road, just like Smokey in his youth.

Smokey hadn't been so keen on the South Wales runs, he was carrying ferrous metal to the steelworks, to the Blast Furnace! He was normally loaded with old railway lines and shoes, or scrap cars. He knew it had to be done, but he could feel the scrap steel quivering uneasily as he entered the gates, it made Smokey and his trailer feel uneasy too. As wheelman drove him down through the plant, he could see the huge crucibles pouring the red hot molten steel, at that point all consciousness was gone. The molten soup being poured to form slabs or bars of red hot steel, ready to be rolled into sheet, bar, or girder. Only then would consciousness begin to return, the cycle continue. Once Smokey had tipped his scrap, he was only too happy to leave the steel plant, wheelman would drive him to a coal head to load best welsh for the return trip. Inside the pit head, the freshly dug coal was running along conveyor belts, loading railway trucks. Wheelman would reverse Smokey's trailer against the first truck, pushing it out of the way, allowing the coal to fill his trailer. The coal was very excited, it had for three hundred million years been trapped in a coal seam deep beneath the earths surface. Laid down during the Carboniferous period, now suddenly it was free, free from all that pressure, free to do as it pleased. Being exploded out of its seam, then put onto a fast moving conveyor, was like being on a fair ground ride! Then for the first time in three hundred million years, it was given a shower in the wash! The coal couldn't be happier, it leapt into Smokey's trailer with great excitement, what was next, it was all so exciting, but then it would be after three hundred million years in the dark! If the coal had eyes, it would have needed sunglasses on the darkest of days. And so the coal leapt into Smokey's trailer, it was so excited it would spill over the sides. Wheelman would have to climb into the trailer with a shovel in his grippers, level out the coal and try to calm it down. As Smokey set off, he could sense the coal excitedly asking where they were going. He didn't have the heart to tell them the truth, told the coal to sit back and enjoy the ride.

Smokey and his wheelman tried to make it a memorable journey for the coal, there was after all no return run! And so Smokey's wheelman would drive as fast as he could, down through the gearbox on the hills, using the two speed axle to split the shifts and keep the Smokey rolling. Then rush down the other side as fast as possible. If there were no bends at the bottom, wheelman would knock Smokey into neutral, let gravity pull the truck along 60 plus mph! Use the momentum to fly back up the next hill, wheelman grabbing top gear as soon as the speed allowed, then full throttle. Rushing around the corners and dropping gears to keep control of Smokey, the coal loved it, flying up and down the hills, the centrifugal force on the corners. It had never been so free, never felt such movement, Smokey tried to give the coal the best ride ever. After a few hours Smokey arrived at the coal yard and tipped his trailer, the coal rushed out with a roar, forming into a heap on the ground. It was still so excited by all these new experiences, 'what's next,' it kept asking Smokey. He told the coal to wait for the next ride, and then left. Smokey didn't have the heart to tell the coal that the next ride was a short one. To a furnace or fire grate, to be heated and then burned, turned to heat, Carbon dioxide, and Sulfur dioxide. Smokey could have told the coal that it was going to be very useful, and then vanish, but Smokey didn't think the coal would be too impressed after waiting three hundred million years in the dark!

15. FRIENDS RESTORED

And so Archie got to know his new compatriots, like him they had been worked hard, as all motors are. They had been fortunate, fallen into the grippers of restorers, this had in part been due to the breaker wheelmen. They didn't want to see the old machines scrapped, carefully kept them to one side until a restorer could be found.

Work on Pop proceeded at a pace, his chassis needed some new steel plates fabricated, then welded in place. The wheelmen were masters of their art, they could turn a flat steel plate into whatever shape was required to fit. Pops axles, gears, and steering box were in good condition, they just needed fresh oil, his wheel bearings packing with new grease. Steering swivels were a different matter, the wheelmen made new steel swivel pins and phosphor bronze bushes on their workshop lathe. Much to Archie's surprise, steering ball joints for Pop were still available, brake shoes however were not. This wasn't a problem for the multi-talented wheelmen, they stripped the shoes and riveted on new linings, his brake drums were skimmed, new clevis pins fitted in his brake rods.

Pops heart, his 1172cc flathead, was a different matter. That was pulled out and dismantled, his crankshaft reground and new bearings fitted, his bores honed, new rings fitted on his pistons, inlet and exhaust valves cleaned and reground. Then all put back together with new gaskets. Pops carburettor, dynamo, distributor and starter motor just needed a clean and were bolted back on. All in all Pop was very happy, as were his parts, many of which had remained with him. He had lost a few engine parts, steering swivels and ball joints, but these parts knew their time was up. They looked forward to after the Blast Furnace, and a new consciousness.

Pops body was next, the badly oxidized parts cut out and new steel welded in, this was uncomfortable for reasons previously explained, but it was the only way to restoration. Pops body was then filled and shaped, primed and given its final coat of gleaming black gloss. His door cards and seats were cleaned and refitted, the wheelmen couldn't contain their surprise at how well they had lasted! The chrome door handles just needed a polish, the thermosetting window surrounds a coat of clear varnish. Once the headlining was cleaned and new carpets fitted, Pop was finished!

Pop was wheeled out into the sunshine, he felt like new, never thought he would ever have that feeling again. The wheelmen were rightly proud of their work, they kept squeezing each others grippers and showing their front piece cutters to one another, Archie and all the other motors had to agree, Pop was top notch!

Work next began on Smokey, aside from his blown piston he was in reasonable condition. He was pressure washed and allowed to drip dry in the sun, then wheeled into the workshop. In no time the wheelmen had him up on axle stands, and his wheels off. Aside from his engine, he was given fresh oil and grease all round. His brakes which were air over hydraulic, were stripped, new seals fitted, shoes re-lined, drums skimmed and the system bled. Work then began on his engine, the head was taken off and sump dropped, which on Smokey could be done with the engine in place. Number three piston had blown and was removed, the rest were fine, the cylinder was honed, and a new piston and rings fitted. The head and sump were replaced, new injectors fitted, fresh oil and filters all around, Smokey was ready to be fired up. It took some cranking before he slowly started to come to life. Then suddenly all six cylinders got their act together, welcomed the new boy in their midst, and gave the crack that only a normally aspirated six cylinder diesel can. Smokey felt brilliant, it was great to be back, the fresh diesel pumping through his injectors, the clean air rushing through his air cleaner, it was some years since he had felt the rush! The wheelmen let his engine warm up on a fast idle, checking for leaks, looking and listening for any problems. There were none, these wheelmen knew their stuff, they checked his brakes were operating, then gently drove him around the yard. Smokey was on cloud nine, it had been so long since he had turned a wheel under his own power, heard the song of his in line six. The wheelmen were very happy, Archie could tell this as they were punching each others gripper sticks with their grippers. He had realised over the years that this could mean either happy or angry, today it was most certainly happy. Smokey was then driven back into the workshop where work then began on preparing him for his paint. Once this was done, he was blasted with red paint on his chassis and wheels, dark blue on his cab, to match Trevor and Archie. The wheelmen then only had to clean the cab seats and interior, and Smokey was ready for his road test. He was relieved he hadn't lost many of his parts, those that had to go knew it, as did Smokey. They made their peace with him as they were removed and put into the scrap bin. The parts had enjoyed their time with Smokey, it had been a good partnership, they had been around for longer than some whilst retired in the corner of the haulage yard. Number three piston in particular had a good chat with Smokey, he was very apologetic, it was after all he that had caused Smokey to be retired. Smokey reassured number three, he had been a solid worker, along with his five compatriots they had covered many thousands of hard worked miles. The blow up was just one of those things, at least Smokey hadn't been sold on, his custodian had kept him safely in the yard. If number three hadn't blown, they may have all ended their consciousness in the Blast Furnace many years ago. Number three agreed, he took heart from what Smokey and the other parts had imparted to him. Now he could go off to the smelting plant, safe in that knowledge, ready to set off on the journey to a new beginning.

The two wheelmen climbed aboard Smokey and took him out for his road test, he felt good, to hit the road again after so many years, was beyond anything that he had ever expected. These wheelmen were good, they had a love of older motors, kept them where they should be, on the road! The wheelman drove Smokey well, he understood the workings of the Eaton two speed, made smooth changes with his Turner five speed box, gently bedding in his rebuilt brakes and the new boy, number three piston. The wheelmen were very pleased with their work, they brought Smokey back into the yard, and parked him amongst the other motors. Archie and the others agreed that Smokey looked very grand, but there was an issue troubling them which they needed to consider!

They all agreed that the yard was getting full, that the wheelmen were going to have to make room for more renovations. Wheelmen exchanged petrol tokens whenever a motor moved from one custodian to another, these wheelmen must have given out lots of them. To keep on renovating old motors, they were going to need a big wedge of new tokens! They rightly guessed that one of them would have to be moved on.

The wheelmen were walking amongst the motors, their renovations, they were looking downcast. After a while they stopped in front of Archie, gave him a friendly but sad tap on the bonnet with their grippers. Archie heard the words, 'this one will have to go,' before they walked away. Archie thought that he might be the one, the wheelmen had Trevor, and Smokey could easily pull Gordy the recovery trailer. Archie was surplus to requirements, he also knew that in his current condition, the wheelmen would get a good wedge of petrol tokens for him. A few days passed before one of the wheelmen brought a tyre kicker to have a look at Archie, only on this occasion, no tyre kicking took place. The tyre kicker walked all around Archie checking his paintwork, opened his bonnet and checked his oil, climbed inside and checked out his seats and even his seat belts! Then wheelman took the tyre kicker for a drive in Archie, showed him how the high and low box and difflock worked. He drove Archie slowly and smoothly, then gave Archie some stick, to show the tyre kicker what Archie could do. The tyre kicker was impressed, Archie heard the words, 'nice old tool,' 'you've done a good job,' and 'it's a flyer.' Archie gathered from this that the tyre kicker was impressed. On returning to the yard, Archie was parked over an inspection pit, the tyre kicker descended, spent some time checking out Archie's underpinnings. Archie then saw wheelman and the tyre kicker shaking grippers before the tyre kicker left. Archie sensed that wheelman was both happy and sad, he also knew that he was on the move, to a new custodian.

That evening, as with previous occasions, Archie was parked up with the other motors, all of whom had become his friends, kindred spirits in this world ruled by wheelmen. They chatted and wished each other well, sorry that one of their number had to move on, they knew it was the way of things. Some of these friends Archie had seen restored back to mechanical perfection by the skill of the wheelmen, as had he. And yet wheelmen were quite often the tools of a motor's destruction, sometimes of themselves! Archie thought it a shame that wheelmen couldn't be a bit more like motors, the world would be a better, safer place!

16. FAMILY

A few days later the tyre kicker returned, he had a lady wheelman with him, together with two miniatures. Archie noticed that the lady wheelman was particularly ball shaped between her gripper sticks and pedal pumper sticks. He had gathered over the years that this meant a new, and very small miniature was imminent. Particularly since when the lady wheelman moved on her pedal pumpers, it was with a rolling gait, this confirmed his suspicions beyond any doubt!

The tyre kicker handed over a wedge of petrol tokens to Archie's wheelman, there was then a further squeezing of grippers, before Archie's wheelman gave him a final pat on the bonnet and walked away. The tyre kicker was now Archie's new custodian and wheelman. The miniatures were carefully strapped in the back, and wheelman helped his lady wheelman into her seat, being particularly concerned for her comfort. Wheelman then climbed up behind the wheel, fired up Archie's V8, dropped him into gear, and gently let out the clutch. Archie could sense that the new wheelman was nervous, felt the vibration through his grippers and his pedal pumpers. More importantly, he could sense the pride of the wheelman, that he had custodian ship of Archie, this was a very good situation for a motor, Archie was pleased. He could also sense the excitement of the two miniatures and the lady wheelman, that Archie was theirs. Wheelman drove smoothly, getting to know Archie, when it was best to change gear, getting the feel of his brakes and steering. Archie realised that he had responsibility for the safety of Wheelman and his family. He wasn't a test bed, work hack, or tow truck, although he had enjoyed all if those roles. Now thanks to the efforts of the wheelmen who had restored him, he was going to be a family vehicle! He had never been one of those before, it was a great responsibility, particularly with two miniatures and a new miniature imminent, Archie was chuffed.

He arrived at his new home, a smallish wheelman shelter in a small town, Archie was parked on a short driveway that led to a lock-up. His new wheelman's shelter was small by comparison with the shelters of his previous custodians. Yet it must be big enough for his new family, and one imminent new miniature. Archie was surprised that some wheelman needed such big shelters, yet others did not, he suspected he was in for a few changes. On arrival, the whole family got out and stood in front of Archie, first wheelman, and then lady wheelman, flashed a bright light at him and the family group. Archie had experience of this, he could sense parts of the light box reforming themselves to form an image of the moment. Wheelmen, Archie realised, liked to capture moments in time which they could keep, to look at in the future with their light receptors. They could then live the moment again, it was like time travel, backwards. Archie had noticed that as clever as wheelmen were, they had not yet managed to produce images of future events. That would be time travel, forwards. This was currently, as far as he was aware, outside the ability of any wheelman. Archie thought that this was a good thing. Otherwise wheelman would know in advance to avoid certain situations, they would only do the good things. This would be bad, as sometimes good things result from bad situations, if you get Archie's drift. Put another way, if Archie had managed to avoid the breakers yard, he would never have been in the custody of the wheelmen renovators. Never have been restored, never have come to be in the custody of his new wheelman, and never have been a family vehicle!

Once Archie's new family had finished capturing the images on the light box, they went inside their shelter, wheelman returned a short while later to give him one more pat on the bonnet.

Archie settled down to survey his surroundings, it was quiet now, he could sense the presence of other motors nearby. They were nothing to do with his wheelman though, they had custodians of their own, and many were family vehicles. Archie had never experienced this before, he had always had friends, to whom he was very loyal, never responsibility as such, it worried Archie, he hoped he would do a good job.

17. NEW ARRIVAL

Archie was woken from his sleep by the sudden banging of doors, and the sound of wheelmen rushing about on their pedal pumpers. He was a bit disorientated at first, this was his first night at his new home. He had woken up staring at a closed up and over door, which was not something Archie was accustomed to. The wheelmen were plainly very excited about something, his wheelman had been banging at the door of the adjoining shelter. Archie thought that the wheelman's stick and core covers were very flimsy, they hardly did the job, and his pedal pumpers had no covers at all! Archie heard the words 'hurry it's on its way,' and 'oh, how exciting.' A lady wheelman wearing similarly ineffective stick and core covers, rushed from the neighbouring shelter, into wheelman's shelter. Archie had his suspicions that the new miniature wheelman might be on its way, he had never been involved in such a thing before, but he had heard that miniatures liked to arrive under the cover of darkness.

Archie's wheelman appeared at the door of his shelter, he had his lady wheelman with him, together with a worried look on his front piece. The lady wheelman was swaying from side to side to such a degree as she walked, Archie thought it amazing she made any forward progress at all! Then there was the sound accompaniment, the lady wheelman was obviously in some pain. He had heard similar from the French policeman, when he had parked on the fellows pedal pumper, but that was a different situation altogether, Archie had been quite pleased about that, now he felt very concerned, it was the responsibility thing. He heard wheelman say 'don't worry, it will be ok,' and 'we must hurry.' Archie thought that the former was most definitely incorrect, whilst the latter was a gross understatement. Archie was all set to launch.

Archie's front passenger door was thrown open, a small wooden box thrown onto the driveway and offered to the lady wheelman as a step. He thought that wheelman was being very caring as he tried to heft his lady wheelman into Archie. It was a struggle, the lady wheelman was like a very large ball with sticks attached, Archie didn't realise that wheelmen could morph to such a size and not explode! He thought that he should help matters along, motors only ever do this times of emergency, or in the case of the French policeman, irritation, oh, and the cattle truck, outright fear! Archie let his springs sense that he wished them to settle, lower his ride height, his leaves had been fully aware of the situation, with all the commotion they could hardly miss it. They gently settled, it was imperceptible, wheelman didn't notice as he was too concerned with lady wheelman. As soon as wheelman had slammed the passenger door, Archie's springs eased themselves back to the correct ride height, they were quite pleased with themselves, wheelman hadn't noticed at all. If he had, his receptors would immediately go into denial, Archie and all fellow motors agreed this was very good, the denial thing. It gave them a bit of leeway, to try and save a situation caused by a wheelman having a moment.

In the meantime, Archie was braced for the lady wheelman's imminent explosion! Wheelman jumped into the drivers seat and fired up Archie's V8, reversed him out of the drive, into first, lots of throttle and dropped Archie's clutch. Archie could tell that wheelman was in a hurry, his V8 started to cough, too much throttle and choke on a cold engine. Fortunately wheelman realised, opened Archie's choke before hitting second gear and max throttle. Archie got the message, as did his Stromberg's, and every other part of him for that matter. He took his responsibilities seriously, always had done, even more so now with a family to look after. Archie made sure that his two Stromberg's gave the smoothest flow of mixture, his coil the best ever spark, his brakes and springs making sure there were no lockups, and the ride smooth, there was a small miniature yet to arrive, they were all one hundred percent on the job! Wheelman drove like a demon, a smooth one with Archie's assistance, Archie was impressed, this fellow could drive, he could see good times ahead. On arrival at the wheelman repair and arrival centre, Archie's leaves did their imperceptible little trick, and wheelman helped his lady wheelman out. As she gently and slowly swayed across the car park, Archie sensed her look back and smile. He and all his parts felt quite anxious, he had never felt like this before, he was slightly confused, he had never had that feeling before either! Archie decided that the best thing to do was sleep, it was the only way to deal with an indeterminate period of waiting. He had practised that a lot in the breakers yard.

Archie was awoken by wheelman quietly opening his rear passenger door, as he gently helped lady wheelman to climb into the back seat. She was cradling the smallest of miniatures in her arms, Archie could feel the great joy in the spirits of the two wheelmen. He also noticed that the lady wheelman looked considerably smaller, for which Archie was very relieved! Wheelman drove back home to their shelter, Archie sat back and relaxed, left it all to wheelman, no need for any help now, the panic was over.

18. IT'S A JOB

Archie settled into his new routine as a family vehicle, he had to admit it was a much easier life. Every morning his wheelman would drive him out to join a super highway, this Archie presumed was for high speed motoring. None of that here, the road was chocker with lots of other wheelmen and their motors, all headed in the same general direction, but slowly. Sometimes the slowly became stopped, for quite long periods of time on occasion, Archie didn't mind, he just chilled. Not so some of the wheelmen, they would treat it like a challenge, chopping from lane to lane and cutting in front of other motors. Archie thought some of the behaviour was most impolite, as did some wheelmen, who would try and block them. Then occasionally the wheelmen would shout and shake their grippers at each other, it could get quite entertaining. Eventually Archie would arrive at a parking lot, where he would be left for the entire day, wheelman later returning to drive him back to wheelman's shelter. At the weekends Archie would be driven to a very large warehouse. There wheelman would park him outside, he would return some time later with a wheeled cage, laden down with items which Archie recognised as wheelmen's food source. Cereals, vegetables, fruit, and protein of various types, sometimes it would include bottles of brown ethanol based liquid. If taken in excess, this tended to render wheelmen first happy and relaxed, leading to unconscious relaxed, and sometimes angry, this could in turn lead to unconscious, courtesy of another ethanol fuelled wheelman. It was also on these weekend days, that wheelman would load up his family and they would go off on family jaunts.

Archie found however, that these family outings could take some organising, the problem was the miniatures, not them directly you understand, but wheelman's perception of their needs. Take wheelman himself as an example. His needs are quite simple, he requires covers for his core, sticks, and pedal pumpers, occasionally he requires a cover for his receptor holder, particularly if the fibres on top are depleting. During the course of the day he will need sustenance, both solid and liquid, these are easily obtained at the many roadside shelters, which wheelmen erect for that purpose. Lady wheelmen are slightly more complex (authors note, they would be wouldn't they). They require a number of different core covers, finding it difficult to decide which best did the job. This follows through to their pedal pumper covers, some would be almost not worth the bother, as most of the pedal pumper is exposed, others would be all enclosing, very sensible in Archie's opinion. Then there would be the rubber pedal pumper and stick cover combo, brought along in anticipation of an almighty deluge of rain, or simple lack of sunshine. Rain would often cause confusion with the lady wheelman, as to which covers, core or pedal pumper, to use. Not so wheelman, he would generally jam a cover on his receptor holder, and get on with it.

The really difficult bit though is the miniatures, if the sun is out, covers would be put on their cores and their sticks left exposed, for cooling purposes. The wheelmen would then spend some time rubbing sun cream on the miniatures sticks, to protect them from the sun. This sun cream having been purchased from a purveyor of such miracle substance, by the exchange of petrol tokens. The lack of such causing much angst amongst the wheelmen, should the sun decide to shine upon the miniature. Then the wheelmen would bring numerous other core and stick covers, some of them impregnable to water, just in case, and various receptor holder covers. Then, dependent upon the size of the miniature, they require various wheeled carriages, or complicated strapping, with which to attach the miniature to a wheelman's core.

Consideration must then be given to the seating within Archie. When he was assembled, he was equipped with suitably upholstered seats for the wheelmen, in addition he had been fitted with belts, to restrain the wheelmen in these seats. A very sensible move, since wheelmen, through over exuberance, aggression, lack of attention, or lapsing into a dream like stupor, would of occasion, cause their motor to collide with another motor, or, more seriously, an immovable object such as a tree (not advisable), or building. The seat belts were fitted to try and restrain the wheelman in such circumstances, and prevent excessive injury. Archie had seen wheelmen with broken sticks before, and it did not look very comfortable.

Archie had noticed that when the new wheelman had checked him over, he had paid particular attention to the seat belts fitted to all passenger seats. Now he knew why, it was because he was now a family vehicle, he was required to have additional seating to secure the miniatures. This seating, was secured to his original seats by means of his seat belts, and it was into this seating that the miniatures had to be strapped. Archie did wonder why the wheelmen didn't just slow down when they had miniatures on board, but he also knew that wheelmen were always in a rush, and also prone to be somewhat uncoordinated of occasion, so maybe the miniature seats were for the best. Once all these complications had been overcome, Archie and his family were able to set off on the adventure of the day.

The family were very keen on going to look at, and immerse themselves in the sea, Archie wondered if this was because of its healing properties. Archie had heard tales of flying wheelman, whose flying machines had caught fire, burning the wheelman's grippers and front piece. It had been discovered that if these wheelmen crashed into the sea, and then immersed themselves in it, that they repaired more readily, than those who did not! And so Archie would be parked up amongst the other motors, whilst his family unloaded all their paraphernalia, then made off to the edge of the sea. Archie wondered of they were drawn to the sea, because that was where many millions of years previously, they had lived. Not as wheelmen you understand, but as some sort of fish. Archie thought this was a strange phenomenon, but then he was just a motor, who was he to argue?

Archie would sit and watch as his wheelmen sat on and dug holes in the sand. The digging was primarily the occupation of the miniatures, then wheelman would put the miniatures in the hole and bury them. Sometimes all that remained above ground was their receptor holder and grippers, all of the wheelmen family thought this was very funny, particularly when the odd wave got a little too close! With all the digging, Archie thought that it looked like hard work, relaxing that is, wheelman style. Then after a period of this relaxing, the wheelmen would launch themselves into the sea, floating with just their receptor holder visible, sometimes they would even disappear completely beneath the surface! Archie wondered if this was anything to do with the fish thing, wanting to return to their roots, or fins in this case. He could foresee a problem here though, wheelmen tended to cease to function if they remained immersed for too long a period. Archie had seen this occur when he was a test bed in Africa. The locals had been trying to get a preview ahead of the publicity release, he had been deep water wading, fitted out with a snorkel and various other bits of water proofing. Suddenly a particularly persistent local lost his footing, slipping down the riverbank and into the river, he was completely immersed, never to be seen again! At the time there had been a huge disturbance in the water, then completely still with no sign of the local wheelman, despite the efforts of the locals to find him. Archie had thought this very strange, maybe he had managed the roots/fins thing? But then Archie had found Africa a strange place, particularly when a passing log opened a light receptor, gave a wink, then quietly floated on by! Fortunately for Archie's wheelman family, after much immersion, they all returned safely, although of a redder hue, and headed back to their shelter.

Once a year Archie's wheelmen would vacate their regular sturdy shelter for two weeks, and live in a very makeshift affair. Archie noted that this was planned with military precision, the wheelmen having to pack an entire support system into his load area. This would include lots of spare stick and core covers, and all manner of pedal pumper and receptor holder covers. Inflatable platforms for the wheelmen to sleep on, bags into which the wheelmen could insert themselves for this purpose. A heating module on which to cook their food, pots and pans, plates, bowls, cups, knives, forks and spoons, table and chairs and a mini chair for the newest miniature. Then there was the frame and canvas material, which made the shelter itself, it was another example to Archie, of how much effort wheelmen put into relaxing!

Once all of this and the family had been somehow squeezed into Archie, they would set off on a journey of several hours before arriving at their destination, a grassed field! There would then follow a period of frantic activity whilst the temporary shelter was erected, and the wheelmen had in place a fully functional support system. Much smaller than the one they had left at home, but nonetheless functional, Archie thought they might just survive the two weeks!

All of this effort by the wheelmen was in the pursuit of relaxation, and the sun, oh and the sea of course. The problem here was the sun, it must have known when Archie's wheelmen were going on holiday, thought that sounded like a jolly good idea, and decided to have one himself. A holiday that is, not a good idea, because it wasn't, the wheelmen needed the sun above their tent at all times! However, Archie as ever, was very impressed by his wheelmen family, they just never gave up. They had come on holiday to enjoy themselves, and have fun, nothing was going to stop them in this quest, especially a reticent sun. NO! They were going to have fun in spite of the reticent sun, ON YOUR BIKE! So to speak, except louder. Eventually the sun decided to do the decent thing and shine, that is after all what its there for. Then the wheelman family were unstoppable, off came their covers, on went the white sun barrier, out came the football, cricket, kite, volley ball, bikes (Archie forgot to mention they brought bikes as well). And when they were tired of that, they would all go and leap in the swimming pool or sea, to get some immersion action in. Where did they get the energy, Archie felt tired just watching, when they got back home they would be good for nothing! This incessant quest to relax continued for the full two weeks, then it was time to pack it all back into Archie and return home. Archie was quite pleased when he was finally parked facing his up and over door, and all the wheelmen were back in their shelter, it was the most tiring experience he had ever been through, and all he had to do was drive along! Archie decided it was all in the mind, watching the wheelmen family go hyperactive for a full two weeks was more than any motor should be subjected to.

Archie settled back into the regular wheelman routine, he had to admit he quite liked being a family vehicle, and he liked his wheelman family. Archie discovered his wheelman had a passion for old steam engines, as a result, one weekend he found himself parked up overlooking a railway museum. This one was of particular interest, as the exhibits were in full working order, and visitors could have rides. Archie, for obvious reasons, had an affinity with anything mechanical. There was one large and impressive Steam Engine, this was being used to give rides around the museum. Archie began to scan the engine, trying to find its consciousness, it took a little while before the engine realised the small irritation it had noticed, was in fact Archie. He found out a number of things, the machines name was Steve, and his official description was a 4-6-4T. That's four small wheels at the front, six large driving wheels, and four small wheels at the back, over which the cab and coal bunker were positioned. He had water tanks either side of his boiler, and his driving pistons and rods were mounted externally at the front of his frame, driving the six large wheels. Archie thought this old machine was impressive, so did all the wheelmen who gathered around to watch, as the two wheelmen attended to the machines needs.

Now Archie had been around for some time, of all machines, he thought that large steam engines were like steel dragons. As Steve stood there, the two wheelmen were working hard to tend to his needs. One was labouring tirelessly with a shovel in his grippers, heaving coal into the firebox, tending to the fire to make sure it burned fiercely. The other carefully adjusting various valves in the cab, all the while Steve stood there like a dragon, hissing steam and roaring when the boiler pressure valve blew. Gently panting as the wheelmen dismounted, pouring oil into small reservoirs to keep the great machine supple, then they would mount up in the cab on the dragon's back. One of the wheelmen would move some levers, the machine would roar, start to move forward with a steady beat of its lungs, faster and faster as the steel dragon gained its stride. Archie thought the whole thing was heroic, so did all the wheelmen, including his family who were watching. Archie would have liked to be heroic, although he did think that his V8 sounded pretty good when wheelman put his boot in the bucket!

There was another engine tucked away in one corner, this one was not of great interest to many of the wheelmen, they had after all come to see the steam engines. This engine however was special, and Archie was pleased to see that his wheelman was having a good look around it. Archie had already made his preliminary scan of the old engine, he had discovered that it was a Deltic diesel by the name of Nobby. He explained to Archie with some embarrassment, and due to his location, in hushed tones, that he was one of the very machines which had replaced the great steam dragons. It wasn't his fault, like all machines, his destiny was in the hands of the wheelmen.

Nobby proudly told Archie that he had a very clever engine installed, two in fact, they were opposed piston two stroke supercharged diesels. Like all engines of this type, Nobby explained, it had no cylinder head, no moving valves, and two pistons operating within one cylinder. Now the two pistons in each cylinder are definitely game on, they rush toward each other at considerable speed, only being constrained from colliding with one another and resultant oblivion by the very sensible crankshafts. A crankshaft is sited at either end of the cylinder, and each piston is attached via a connecting rod to its nearest crankshaft, the crankshafts themselves being linked to one common output shaft, and thereby synchronized together. In rushing toward one another, the pistons compress the air within the cylinder and between them, to a very small volume and high pressure. As a result the air molecules so constrained become very hot and most uncomfortable, they just want to float freely around in the atmosphere, as they had been doing a very short time previously. Then, as if it isn't crowded enough already, some very oily and smelly diesel fuel is pumped in to join them in an atomised form. Now the air is definitely peeved, it was after all fresh a few moments before, and the diesel isn't too happy either, it suddenly found itself compressed to one hundred bar, then forced through some incredibly small holes in an injector. So small in fact that the diesel is pretty much atomised, which is enough to put any fuel into a bad mood, then it finds itself in a very enclosed space with very hot and similarly bad tempered air molecules. Needless to say it's not a good introduction, the two just aren't going to get along, the diesel thinks, 'I'm out of here', nicks the airs oxygen and combusts. Well that's not such a good move in such a confined space, the combustion causes a massive heat and pressure rise, which completely changes the form of both the air and diesel. Strangely enough the two combine together, all their differences forgotten, with a view to escaping their confinement. Fortunately at this point in time, the turning crankshafts have reversed the direction of the pistons away from one another, allowing the very angry burning exhaust gases, to force the pistons apart at quite a pace, turning the crankshafts, and losing some of their pent up anger and energy as they do so. Then suddenly freedom beckons, one of the two pistons uncovers an open port in the cylinder wall towards the end of its stroke. The hot exhaust gases, which still have a fair amount of angry energy, seize the opportunity and rush out of this port into the exhaust system and noisy freedom. Now shortly after one piston had opened its exhaust port, the other piston uncovers the inlet ports in its end of the cylinder wall. Now the exhaust gases are in such a rush to get out of the exhaust port, they can't be bothered to change direction and try to get out of the newly opened inlet port. This is just as well, as lurking the other side of the inlet port is some similarly angry compressed air which has been squeezed into the induction manifold. This air was until a few moments earlier, floating happily along in the atmosphere, only to suddenly find itself sucked into an induction pipe, spun around by some closely meshed rotors in the supercharger, and jammed into that induction manifold. It wants some shoulder room. As soon as that inlet port opens, it rushes through into the cylinder and what it thinks is freedom, duly helped by the suction of the exhaust gases rushing out of the exhaust port. Now before the compressed air can make good its escape, those calm and controlling crankshafts, reverse the direction of those two mad as a hatter pistons. Pushing them back toward one another, they are particularly sneaky about it too, making sure that the exhaust port is covered by its piston and closed before the inlet port. The compressed air just keeps on rushing in, thinks its escaping, then the truth dawns, the other piston covers its inlet port. The air knows it is trapped, can sense the two pistons closing in on it, compressing it to a degree which it would much rather not experience. It realises it has been well and truly duped, it will know better next time! In the meantime it's getting pretty hot under the collar, and there is much much less shoulder room than in that induction manifold waiting room. Next minute, surprise surprise, its joined by the angry smelly diesel, as far as the air is concerned matters couldn't get any worse, if only it knew. Then the rather peeved diesel nicks the airs oxygen and combusts, the two combine and expand pushing the pistons apart, and so the two stroke cycle in each cylinder continues. Nobby was particularly proud of his two stroke diesel Deltic engines, each being an eighteen cylinder, thirty six piston, three crankshaft wonder. Nobby told Archie that any wheelman stood nearby when his engine was opened up, could feel the power through his core and pedal pumpers. Archie thought Nobby was a very fine machine, if the Steam Engines were steel dragons, these Deltics were steel monsters! Archie had a good view of the engines at the railway museum, he had enjoyed his conversations with Steve and Nobby, in fact he had thoroughly enjoyed the day, as had his wheelmen. Then Archie's family loaded aboard and headed back to their shelter. They were all in a happy mood, and before long, Archie was parked up in front of his up and over door. Archie was really enjoying being a family motor, apart of course from the weekday job, of taking his wheelman to work, and sitting in jam of other motors. It was the miniatures that did it for Archie though, this was a whole new experience.

19. WHAT ARE THEY LIKE?

Archie knew all about wheelmen, they after all created him, and the whole fabric that he and they existed within. Both Archie, and every other object created by the wheelmen, were subject to the good, bad, and crazy sides of them. It could be a bit disconcerting of occasion, a motor's existence could be severely damaged, or even finished, by a wheelman having a moment. They were like tainted gold, able to create so much from raw materials, and yet also able to destroy, it was enough to make a motor have a breakdown. Motors like all machines and materials, had learned to live with them, enjoy the ride, but be ready, guard against the mad moment which was inevitable. For all their clever ways, wheelmen didn't realise that all materials had a consciousness, this transferred to anything made by the wheelmen, why Archie and all his parts had consciousness. Each part immediately knows its function, a ball joint after all, knows exactly what to do, no question at all. It is because of this, in moments of danger to either the wheelman or machine, that the machine can take control. There are however universal rules, it must be done in a manner the wheelman cannot detect, this is helped by the wheelman's absolute belief, that all objects are inanimate. If his receptors detected any such self-will, they immediately go into denial, a motor still has to use common sense however. If wheelmen were to realise they did not have absolute control of the world, how would they deal with it? It would be a mighty shock to realise that the mirror he was looking at, was actually looking back, and had an opinion! That would possibly make some of them tidy themselves up, or maybe not. Then that double scotch. It was actually thinking 'down the hatch', as it hurtled down inside wheelman's core, Intent on wreaking havoc with his innards. Take heroin as an example, it was existing quite happily inside a poppy flower, wheelman comes along, rips it out of the poppy to make said substance. The heroin is very angry, as soon as it gets inside wheelman, it does its best to make him ill, get its own back. It's the same with potatoes, eat too many of them and a wheelman will become ill. Why does a wheelman feel pain when a falling brick hits him on the receptor holder? It's because the brick is getting its own back. The sand clay and aggregate were quite happy existing in the ground, had done for thousands of years. Then wheelman comes along, digs them up, squeezes them into a mould, and cooks the lot in a very hot oven. It's hardly surprising that the brick wants pay back.

In fact, pretty much the whole world created by wheelmen, would like to return to its constituent parts. Taken any object you care to name, Wheelman's shelter is just waiting to fall on his head. Any sort of bridge you care to mention, suspension, cantilever, or arch. All of them are itching to relax, let all that tension or compression go, and fall in the hole! Wheelmen build machines which are at some moment going to wipe them out. Such an example is the helicopter, they are guaranteed at regular intervals to fall out of the sky. Wheelmen quite like the Wop, Wop, sound, that it makes as it fly's along. If their receptors could hear the rotor blades constituent materials chant, 'not just yet' 'not just yet', or 'got to get the moment right' 'got to get the moment right', they might not be so keen. Wheelmen really do live on a knife point of their own creation.

As you see, Archie was fully clued up about wheelmen, but not the miniatures. It must be said that he was most surprised at how helpless the newest of them were. Archie had spent some time working on farms, experienced young animals of all sorts. All of them, with few exceptions, can pretty much make it on their own from the moment they hit the turf. What can a new miniature do? Archie can testify that mostly squawk, whimper a lot, sleep, and intake nourishment, all whilst under the close supervision of lady wheelman, or wheelman, without whom they would be sunk.

How then, do these helpless and slow developing beings, get to run the show, that's what Archie finds somewhat confusing. They even managed to create him, not his consciousness you understand, that came from his constituent parts which were dug out of the ground some years previously. Archie saw that as the miniatures grew, their ability to communicate and control their movements continually improved. Most notable was the amount they had to learn, and the ability to learn.

That, Archie realised, was the difference between the wheelmen, and every other being on the planet. For the wheelmen to survive in the world they had created, every new wheelman had to learn so much. Not so any other being, they were born with the knowledge and ability to survive, they had a place within the world, did not even think to try and change it. Wheelmen on the other hand, could not possibly survive, if they didn't change the world. They are too weak and frail, they had to change the world to suit their needs in order to flourish. Erect shelters to give them warmth and protection, machines to give them power, enable them to make those changes. The other notable difference between wheelmen and all other beings, they wanted to learn, to try different activities, explore whether a certain objective can be achieved. Archie suddenly found the missing part of the jigsaw that is a wheelman, contentment. They are rarely in that situation, constantly driven on to try and achieve better. Occasionally there would be a moment, and then they would be off again, improving or changing. The quest never ending, until suddenly the wheelman's sticks or core would fail, and they would cease to function.

Archie had noticed that wheelmen had a limited time span of existence. Motors were, if not for oxidation, abuse by wheelmen, or cataclysmic natural event, capable of an infinite existence. Wheelmen on the other hand, tended to cease to function after twenty five thousand five hundred and fifty suns (roughly). Hardly any of them at all, ever exceeded thirty six thousand five hundred suns (roughly). Some, quite often through injudicious behaviour, terminated their existence before reaching ten thousand suns (roughly). And yet they behaved as if their time was infinite, wired not to accept that termination was guaranteed. On the other gripper, maybe it was an acceptance of this fact that drove them to achieve so much, make the most of the short time they had? Archie found this all very sobering, it was enough to give a motor a migraine.

Archie watched as the miniatures grew. The two older ones progressed from wobbling around on their pedal pumper sticks, to racing around like their pedal pumpers were on fire, always a question mark in the air. The newest miniature had grown fast, he was now at the wobbling on his pedal pumper stick stage, not talking as yet, but understanding what the wheelmen said. There was a lot of happiness in this wheelman family, Archie hoped he would continue to be part of it.

And continue it did, in order to heat their shelter, Archie would be driven to the local coal yard. Wheelman would load him up with bagged smokeless, coal that has been well and truly cooked to remove the smokey coal gas. It reminded Archie of the stories told by Smokey the trader, of bringing coal back from the welsh valleys. He could sense the coke, it wasn't full of excitement, it had already been through a coking plant, realised the game was up. Not much Archie could do really, just quietly get on with it, at least give the coke a smooth ride. Archie was used to transport all sorts of materials for wheelman's projects. There was always something to be built or improved, Archie guessed it was the contentment thing.

20. STOLEN

Archie was quietly sleeping in front of the family shelter, he was brought back to consciousness by an implement in his drivers door lock. He recognised immediately that it wasn't his regular key, it had been with him since his parts were first assembled, he knew every indent on that key like the back of his gripper (if he had one). He regularly said good morning or good night, dependent upon the time of day that he was locked or unlocked. This definitely wasn't his key, it was the same sort of shape, but old and worn. Archie could sense an unknown wheelman jiggling it in his lock, trying to get the barrel to turn, the barrel itself knew it was the wrong key, an invader. He was trying his best not to turn, not to let his tumblers line up, the struggle went on for a few moments. Archie sensed the sigh from his lock, realised the tumblers had been aligned, his drivers door was opened. The wheelman jumped into Archie's seat, he felt another steel key inserted in his ignition lock, the jiggling started again. His ignition lock was now engaged in the same struggle as the door lock, unfortunately this wheelman was very practised in the lock jiggling business. Before long, Archie felt his ignition lock give way under the pressure, the barrel turned, Archie's V8 had no option but to start.

This wheelman was clever too, no big throttle opening as Archie's V8 fired, just let it gently tick over. He quietly dropped Archie into reverse, gripper brake off, slowly off of the drive, into first and gently drove Archie away. You may have wondered why Archie didn't intervene, he has in the past. Well, Archie has to abide by universal rules, he cannot interrupt his normal mechanical process unless his wheelman is in danger, or there are compassionate reasons for doing so, or Archie himself is in danger of serious damage due to a moment on behalf of his wheelman. Finally, it must not be recognised by the wheelman that the motor has taken any action. As much as he would have liked to intervene, this situation was outside the guidelines, Archie knew he was on the move, and no petrol tokens had been exchanged.

This was an entirely new situation for Archie, never before had he been in the custody of a dishonest wheelman. More to the point, he was being taken away from his family, Archie was devastated. He hadn't ever felt this way before, all his other wheelmen had just been custodians, he had become quite fond of one or two, but they were just his operators. It was with the other vehicles that he had become friends. It was different for a family vehicle, he liked his family, enjoyed helping them to get along and improve their lives. The holidays and jaunts out, helping wheelman with all his projects, it had been special, Archie was going to miss his family a lot.

Now Archie had a new custodian, he must do this wheelman's bidding, Archie buckled down, time to move on. He felt his V8 warming up, getting into its stride, this wheelman knew how to drive, accelerating his V8 to that sweet spot before up shifting. Archie's V8 was enjoying sucking in all that air, opening his lungs, his Stromberg's enjoying the rush. Family life had been good, but wheelman had been gentle, frugal most of the time. This wheelman was reckless, plainly didn't care, Archie feared he might be in for a hard and dangerous time.

Wheelman hit the super highway, Archie normally crawled along here in a traffic jam, not tonight, wheelman joined the slip road, dropped Archie into third and gave it the beans. Before he knew it, wheelman had hit seventy mph, up-shifted Archie into fourth, then cranked the throttle open again. All of Archie's parts were up for it, his V8 growling, his transmission singing. Archie surged ahead to his wind resisted maximum, of one hundred and five mph. Wheelman kept his pedal pumper planted, this fellow was going to well and truly stretch Archie's pedal pumper sticks!

The thing was, Archie was enjoying it, it was like the early days when Archie was a test bed, being put through his paces. Then Archie heard the police siren, wheelman heard it too, he slowed and pulled Archie off into a side road. He accelerated hard away from the super highway, then threw Archie into an unmade farm track, stopped and turned off Archie's lights. They sat quietly, Archie's V8 gently turning over, he could hear wheelman breathing, patiently waiting. The police car sped past on the super highway, Archie thought briefly of his family wheelman, finding Archie was gone, there was no point, the clock had moved forward.

Wheelman waited for a few minutes, listened as the siren disappeared, then gently reversed Archie back into the side road. Switched on Archie's lights, drove steadily down the road, like Archie's family wheelman on a day out. Wheelman kept to the side roads now, working across country, through farmland. Archie heard a few more sirens at first, that soon stopped, wheelman picked up the pace a little, but not enough to draw attention. He knew where he was going, never any hesitation at junctions. Archie realised he had been targeted, how else would this wheelman know the exact route, keeping off the main highways, all country roads, no people, no cameras.

They drove on for some time, finally wheelman turned off into a farm track, quite narrow and rough, it was no problem for Archie, that was what he was built for. Finally they came to a halt outside a barn, another wheelman was there, he opened the barn doors, Archie was driven inside. The heavy doors were closed behind him, lights flicked on inside. Wheelman switched off Archie's lights and engine, climbed down from Archie, he was joined by the other wheelman, who Archie thought was in charge. They walked around Archie, checking him over. Archie could hear his V8 ticking as it cooled, his bonnet was opened, the two looked at his V8, he heard the words, 'Nice motor, you did well', 'We'll start work on it tomorrow'. Then the two left, switching off the barn lights as they went. Archie settled down for the night, he was having a problem coming to terms with how he felt, as were all his parts. He felt excited, couldn't wait for tomorrow, no more regular nine to five traffic jams Monday to Friday. Archie felt guilty, but then what else was he to do. A motor has to do the bidding of his wheelman, it's just that these wheelmen were different from any other that he had known.

Archie was woken up by the lights flicking on in his barn. Wheelman opened Archie's bonnet and started work straight away, checked his oil and water, removed and reset his spark plugs. Cleaned and set the points in his distributor, checked his fan belt and radiator hoses. Archie realised wheelman was making sure he wouldn't let them down, he guessed that whatever was going to happen, the man in the yellow van wasn't going to be involved. Then wheelman jacked Archie up and removed all his wheels, adjusted his brakes so they were perfect. Replaced his wheels and tyres with new ones, Archie could sense they were aggressive, confident, puncture proof! Archie had heard about these tyres, never thought he would need anything like it, he guessed these wheelmen weren't going to stop for anything. Then he greased Archie's propshaft universal joints, checked the oil levels in his axles and transmission, finally he checked that all of Archie's lights worked.

Archie was impressed, this fellow was a deft hand with the spanners, thorough too, he realised what this was all about. The wheelmen wanted him on the mark, and they didn't want him to attract attention, so no dodgy bulbs, no reason to be stopped by a policeman. Wheelman finally changed Archie's number plate, he had a new identity, was under the radar. Wheelman walked around Archie, giving him the once over, a last kick of his tyres, then he slipped into Archie's drivers seat, and turned the key. Archie's V8 fired immediately, wheelman waited for it to warm up, opened the choke and blipped the throttle. Archie's V8 responded sweeter than ever, wheelman was pleased, he tapped Archie's steering wheel with his gripper, 'Nice one'. Archie thought so too.

Mainman walked into the barn, over to Archie, he put his gripper stick around wheelman's core, then punched him twice with his other gripper. They showed their front piece cutters to one another and laughed, both wheelmen then got to work on Archie, carefully darkening his windows with tinting film. Archie was surprised at himself, he knew these wheelmen were up to no good, potentially he could end up in the Blast Furnace, but he felt safe in their grippers, they were capable, skilled with the spanners. He might survive, when the job is done go back to his family, he would certainly have a tale to tell. In the meantime he prepared himself, as did all his parts, they were up for the challenge. The wheelmen then removed his front bumper, replaced it with a heavy duty 'get out of my way affair'. It had a remote control eleven thousand pound winch attached, with thirty meters of steel cable. Wheelman wired this in, and fitted a brake light kill switch, whilst mainman welded on a 'get out of my way', three inch square steel box section to Archie's rear crossmember.

Wheelman climbed aboard Archie, fired up his V8 and reversed him out of the barn, it was daylight now. Archie could see derelict farm buildings, pretty much in the middle of nowhere. Wheelman gently drove Archie back down the track to the side road, his V8 was running on the sweet spot, his brakes perfect, but he felt heavier. Once on the tarmac, wheelman checked Archie was up to temperature, then hit the gas, accelerating hard through every gear, keeping his pedal pumper planted. The road was straight for some distance, Archie hit eighty five mph before wheelman had to lift, but Archie knew he was slower, it was the extra weight. Wheelman didn't seem to mind the lack of pace, he was whistling, happy. He turned Archie around and headed back to the farm, driving gently now, relaxed. They rolled into the barn, mainman was there, Archie heard the words, 'Good?' followed by, 'yeah good, need to fit the nitrous, need about fifty brake.' Wheelman set to work straight away, fitting a nitrous kit.

Like the tyres, Archie had heard of Nitrous, knew it was heady stuff, instant power increase, but it could blow a motor apart. He was concerned for his engine, provided the wheelman stuck with a fifty bhp increase, his V8 should survive. This whole venture was on the limit, risky, a fifty bhp increase, that would definitely get him moving, provided his pistons didn't melt! The job was finally done, wheelman took Archie out for another blast, it went well. Wheelman was impressed, so was Archie, his V8 was particularly happy, he was still in one piece, survived all that heat in his combustion chambers, all that extra pressure. Archie was driven back to the barn, parked up, the lights turned off, barn doors locked, it made him laugh, these fellows were very security conscious! Archie settled down for the night, he needed to rest, he was starting to feel a little nervous.

It was a lazy start to the day for Archie, he had woken as usual, but the barn was still in darkness, quiet. No sign of any wheelmen, Archie felt apprehensive, it was different. The wheelmen had been putting in the hours on him, now he was ready to go. Archie realised that was the key, he was ready to go!

Darkness had descended on the barn, there was no light filtering in through the gaps in the roof tiles. The barn lights flicked on, Archie saw the two wheelmen and a third, a new one, he was different to the others, smaller, younger, his grippers small and slender. They walked over to Archie, the younger wheelman opened his bag, pulled out a file of paperwork, laid it on Archie's front wing. Archie could sense the ink on the papers, it was quite new, lots of lines criss-crossing the pages, lots of symbols which he didn't understand. The ink didn't have any information to pass to Archie, it never did, ink just made the mark, never understood what the mark meant. That after all wasn't its job, all it had to do was be tidy, never ever run, and don't fade, if ink did that, job done. But there was more to ink than you would think, it was like having an undercover agent in on the job, at least it was if you were Archie.

Archie delved deeper, seeking the consciousness of the ink, he knew it would be there, just a bit reticent, secretive. Archie needed to get on side, appeal at an atomic level, material to material. The ink responded, what did Archie want? Get to the point, the ink just wanted to quietly dry, become fully one with the paper, it didn't need any distractions. Archie asked the ink what it had heard the wheelman say, as he was drawn, line by line onto the paper. The ink said it didn't understand any of it, they were just noises to him. Archie knew he was onto a winner, just repeat the noises it asked the ink, then I will leave you alone. The ink sighed, this sort of thing didn't happen very often, if the ink was really honest, it had never happened, not to him. He could sense that Archie wasn't going to let go, better get it over with, then the ink could concentrate on drying. The ink passed over the vibrations stored within its atoms, it meant nothing to the ink, but Archie understood. It's not possible to exist alongside the wheelmen as long as Archie had, and not learn to understand what all these gasps of air meant. Archie felt the vibrations, understood and changed them into words. Central bank, underground services, telephone lines, alarm system, deactivate, ghost system, it can be done, no problem, we're in then, job's on. Archie understood, the new wheelman was the techie, it was a bank job, and he was going to ghost the alarm system.

The wheelmen started to load Archie with equipment, two pry bars, two sledge hammers, bolt croppers, heavy duty work gloves, two pairs night vision goggles, four large canvas holdalls, a framework with attachment points, percussion drill and bits, fixing bolts, hydraulic drive unit, petrol powered hydraulic pump, small petrol generator and lighting set, two breathing sets. Archie had never seen some of the equipment before, but he could tell it was all top quality. There were also three large cylindrical cutters fitted with diamond teeth. Archie could sense their aggression, it made Archie feel uncomfortable. Not as uncomfortable as the last item though, a portable oxy/acetylene cutting set. Archie knew he was safe from this though, they were hardly going to cut him up, he was part of the plan, one of the gang. No worries there, Archie always gave his wheelman one hundred percent, whatever the circumstances.

21. LAWLESS

The three wheelmen shook grippers, Archie could sense they were excited, apprehensive, fully focused on the job in hand. Archie's petrol tank was brimmed, they gave his tyres one last kick, like a team high-five before they hit the field. Then the three set their time pieces, the young techie wheelman left. Wheelman climbed aboard Archie, fired up his V8, gently tapped Archie's dashboard with his gripper. Mainman opened the barn doors, Archie crept out into the darkness, the barn lights flicked off, barn doors closed. Mainman climbed aboard, Archie sensed the two wheelmen communicating with their light receptors, a gentle nod of their receptor holders. Wheelman eased out Archie's clutch, they were off, the job was on.

Wheelman drove gently, cutting across country, not drawing attention, they hit the super highway, up to speed, match the traffic flow, blend in. Archie felt secure, different number plate, wheels, front bumper, rear bumper and a winch. He was a different motor now, with a very different purpose. He could sense the nitrous quietly waiting to work its magic, all of Archie's parts felt it, his V8 in particular, anxious that the nitrous didn't finish him. And so it continued, closer into town, the wheelmen said nothing, Archie could feel their tension, hear their quiet breathing. Onward they drove, passing houses, shops, retail units, office's, past warehousing and industrial units, new, old, derelict. They came to a roundabout, wheelman pulled off into a service road, gently, no fuss. Onward again, more warehousing, derelict, empty, uncared for, forgotten. Wheelman pulled Archie into a derelict site, drove between the derelict buildings, lights off, carefully, slowly in the darkness. Archie could sense that the wheelman had been here before, they drove down a narrow alley, to their left, a long since disused warehouse. The bricks in the building had seen better times, now they knew they were for the crusher, resigned to their fate. They sensed Archie, then the wheelmen, hadn't seen any of those in a while. Sensed the tension, it roused the bricks from their torpor, something of interest, they watched.

Wheelman drove almost to the end of the alley, Archie heard mainman, 'It's just ahead, stop here'. Wheelman quietly stopped, turned Archie's engine off. Several meters ahead, and to Archie's right, a reinforced concrete parapet. It had a job to do, but it wasn't making a fuss, or shouting how important it was, holding the river back, keeping the town from flood. The ever searching pressure of the water, as the river tried to find a weakness in the wall, regain its flood plain, long since stolen by wheelmen. Then it could rest, take its time, not the constant rush through the narrow trench, made by the wheelmen when they stole the rivers land. Archie could hear the angry river, sense the curiosity of the old bricks, he felt uncomfortable, intruding. The two wheelmen pulled covers over their receptor holders, put on the night vision goggles, checked their time pieces. Archie could sense they were waiting for a window in time, never to be repeated, like a time traveller, except the wheelman's time was now. They both moved, quietly, decisively, working to a plan, each wheelman knowing what to do. They took the equipment out of Archie, placing it on the floor in front of him, quietly, quickly. Archie was scanning the roadway ahead of him, it had been there a long time, a shaft, its bricks older than those in the derelict building. Built when wheelmen stole the flood plain, Archie explored from brick to brick, seeking an explanation from each. None of them knew their purpose, other than to lie there on top of the brick below, keeping the structure of the square shaft. At each question Archie was told, 'Ask him, I don't know why I'm here', so Archie scanned deeper brick by brick, finally reaching the bottom twenty meters down. Archie had his answer, a tunnel leading under the river, disused but still there, dry, a river crossing, out of sight, out of mind. Archie could only guess where it led, as for the bricks, they told him nothing, even the ones in the tunnel. Archie had heard wheelmen use the term, 'Thick as a brick', now he knew why.

The wheelmen took their pry bars, opened the steel cover on the shaft, it opened quietly, smoothly, oiled. The wheelmen had been here already, lubricated the old hinges, preparation, planning, execution. They wound out Archie's winch with the remote, mainman went down first, with the lighting set and generator. Wheelman lowered the rest of the kit down, finally winching himself down the shaft and out of sight. Archie sat quietly in the darkness, his winch wound out twenty meters, no sleeping this night though, Archie was tight as a bow string. Until his wheelmen returned this was his spot, just the sound of the river, always searching for a weakness, to keep him company.

Archie was jerked back to attentiveness by the sirens and flashing blue lights, it was on the other side of the river, directly opposite Archie. He was concerned, what could he do, sit quiet, wait. Archie's winch started, he could feel there wasn't much weight, it was winching in fast. There was just one wheelman, no kit, no mainman, and wheelman was very wet. Wheelman wound in the winch, climbed aboard Archie, fired up his V8. He was breathing hard, the way he dropped Archie's clutch as he reversed out of the dead end, he wasn't cool or controlled. Archie heard the words 'damn roof', and 'tunnel flooded', he put it all together. Just before the sirens and the lights, he had heard the river, louder than before, excited, triumphant. It had found a weakness and broken through, thought it could take back its flood plain. The river was wrong, it had broken through, but all it had taken back was the tunnel, flooded the tunnel and shafts. Either mainman was trapped on the other side, or trapped in the tunnel. Whichever way, Archie knew that wheelmen couldn't remain immersed for long, they ceased to function.

22. PURSUIT

Archie could sense wheelman's pain, his loss, he felt it too, motors become attached to their wheelmen, it doesn't matter who their wheelman is, or what he does. Wheelman turned Archie around and headed for the gate. He wasn't driving carefully, wasn't trying to blend in and not be noticed, he was driving to get away, distance himself from whatever had happened in the tunnel. Archie knew it was wrong, they would show out, but what could he do, wheelman was driving hard, wanted speed and distance. Archie and all his parts delivered, his V8 on song as ever, perfectly set up by wheelman.

They launched out of the gate onto the roadway, headed out of town. Archie's tyres scrabbled for grip as wheelman turned and accelerated at the same time, his balance unsettled by the ramp onto the roadway. Wheelman was winding Archie up in every gear, a thirty mph limit, they hit seventy in third. Archie saw it turning out of a side road, slowly, its policeman searching, a police car.

As Archie flashed by he felt his wheelman tense, his grippers tighten on Archie's steering wheel. The Blue lights and two tone horn started, the headlights of the SD1 police car rising as its policeman hit the throttle. Archie could sense the police motor, nothing personal, it's what I do, its V8 motor the same as Archie's, working hard, giving its all. Archie knew they were in with a shout, he had nitrous, but he would still top out at one hundred and fifteen mph. The other police cars would be homing in, wheelman buckled down, whatever had happened in the tunnel, his whole attention was on the matter in hand, driving Archie.

Wheelman knew the way, accelerating hard, left and right, using the nitrous to put space between Archie and the police car. Trying to get out of town, but not onto the super highway, Archie would be a dead duck. Get out onto the country roads, wheelman knew them well, practised, lots of bends, acceleration needed, Archie had plenty of that. Archie felt wheelman's confidence rise as they hit the unlit roads. Then he pulled his last ace out of the pack, put on his night vision goggles, killed Archie's lights, hit the brake light kill switch, game on. Wheelman pushed ever harder, getting his rhythm, Archie's V8 was breathing hard, his Stromberg's gulping air as fast as they could. On full throttle the nitrous kicked in, Archie's V8 knew he could cope with it now, wasn't going to blow. He was confident, waiting for the rush as the nitrous and extra fuel hit him, the heat, the pressure, the extra power as he forced Archie on quicker and quicker. Archie's gears were singing their song as wheelman hit max revs in every gear, he was no longer just operating Archie now, the sound of Archie had found wheelman's soul, he was part of the machine now, he and Archie were one.

The police cars started to fall behind, their crews didn't know the area, couldn't see Archie's outline in the darkness. Archie felt Wheelman braking hard in the darkness, no lock ups, wheelman wasn't going to leave any clues. He turned gently into a rough and narrow track, picking up speed gently, careful not to throw gravel out onto the road, to show where he had gone as he disappeared into the darkness of the fields.

The sounds of the police sirens diminished, their lights disappearing as they chased shadows. Wheelman gently picked his way along the lane, the two now no longer one, but still working together, smoothly, wheelman and motor. The hedges closed in, scraping at Archie's paintwork, they were in tractor country now, no cars allowed. Archie definitely wasn't one of those, wheelman hit the difflock, dropped Archie into second and opened the throttle. Archie was in his element as wheelman pushed him cross country.

They drove for some time before finally arriving back at the barn, the slim wheelman, the techie, was there. He opened up the barn doors as they arrived, wheelman drove inside, the doors closed as wheelman killed Archie's V8, the barn lights flicked on. Wheelman tapped Archie's steering wheel, 'well done', but Archie could sense there was sadness, loss. Wheelman climbed down from Archie, he was joined by the young techie, Archie sensed even more sadness here. The two put their grippers around each others cores, held each other for a moment, silent. Archie realised mainman wasn't coming back, whatever had happened in that tunnel had been final.

Wheelman started to organise them both, he reversed a Ford van into the barn, they loaded their tools and equipment, clearing the barn of any trace. Then they wiped Archie down, not to clean him, just remove any trace of themselves, removed the false plates and refitted Archie's real number. Archie knew his adventure was over, wheelman gave Archie's bonnet a farewell tap with his clenched gripper. The young techie pulled the van out of the barn, the lights flicked off, the barn doors shut and locked, security. Archie listened as the Ford drove away, its noise disappearing, he felt sad and alone. Wheelmen always surprised him, he had seen that hidden side again as they mourned mainman. He had felt it himself, even though they had stolen him from his family, the time spent with them had been intense. Archie had been through the grippers of many wheelmen, but this was the first time one of them had lost his consciousness, ceased to exist. It was a new experience for Archie, he had to admit he didn't much like it, Archie decided the best way was to sleep, he shut down, darkness enveloped him.

23. POTATOES

Archie remained in that barn undisturbed for two years. During that time he became home to numerous rodents and insects, gathered a good covering of dust, bird and bat droppings. The leaking barn roof helping to add to his general dishevelment, together with the dents and scratches he had gained whilst escaping across the fields. Archie was only found when wheelman was caught, and thought that he might as well spill the beans on Archie's hiding place, wipe the slate clean so to speak. Wheelman wasn't so upset about going to prison either, he got to join his brother mainman, who hadn't ceased to exist at all.

The two had made a mistake with their tape measure in the darkness of the tunnel, drilled into the bottom of the river, instead of the bottom of the central bank. Wheelman had been at the bottom of the shaft leading up to Archie when the deluge of water hit him. Mainman had been taken completely by surprise, by his unexpected and very sudden immersion from above. He managed to get to his nearest vertical shaft, climbing the steel rungs as fast as he could, whilst the river chased his pedal pumpers. This brought him out via a steel cover, into the roadway to one side of the bank. It was quite a surprise to the policeman, as mainmans very wet receptor holder and core, suddenly appeared in the glare of his police motors headlamps.

The fact that the bank alarm had gone off at all was a mystery to mainman. His son, the young techie wheelman, was a very clever fellow. He had quite correctly disabled, and then ghosted the Central banks alarm system. What he hadn't done was disable the alarms in the two adjoining banks, the Left bank, and the Right bank, there was after all no need. Unfortunately, the very excited river, in the mistaken belief it was going to get its flood plain back, had rushed into the conduits holding all three banks telephone cables. This set off the alarm to the Left bank, and the Right bank, not the Central bank you understand, as young wheelman had done his job absolutely spot on.

Mainman was hauled away by the policemen, dried off, and eventually sent to prison for quite an extended period. He didn't let on about his brother wheelman, or his son, young techie wheelman, not until two years later that is. All the prisoners were celebrating the prison governors birthday, mainman having drunk far too much illegal hooch, which he had brewed on the prison potato patch. In his inebriated state, he had told a fellow prisoner of the bank job, of wheelman, and of young wheelman. The receiver of this information was something of a gossip, and sadly to say, prison snitch. Word soon reached the prison governor of this hitherto unknown information. This in turn led to wheelman, and young techie wheelman, being rounded up, put in irons, and Archie's location revealed.

It was the bright sunlight that brought him around, and the voices. Archie was very confused, apart from the odd conversation with either a rat, mouse, spider or nesting bird, (and they were odd conversations). Archie hadn't had contact with any being, mechanical or otherwise. Suddenly his doors were being opened, there were wheelmen, and they were wearing white coveralls, masks and rubber gloves. It was all very disconcerting, and there were several similarly attired wheelmen, all poking around both Archie and his barn. After three or four suns, (Archie lost track here), he was hauled away on the back of a low loader. Archie tried to find out from the low loader what was happening, where he was going, but the low loader had taken some sort of oath of silence, wouldn't tell Archie anything, got all superior. Archie thought, fair enough, gave the wink to his most trusted resident rodent, explained the situation regarding his security of tenure, and why it was at an end. Stan (the rodent), had been very comfortable in amongst Archie's seat cushions, thought the low loader needed to learn a little humility. He hopped down onto the load bed, was going to hide out in the low loaders chassis rails, sneak out at night, and give the motors engine loom a good chewing. If Stan had been a wheelman, he would have been top notch with the spanners.

After a fairly lengthy drive, they arrived at a secure pound operated by policemen, Archie was unloaded from the low loader, who, being aware of Stan, was trying to get onside. Archie was having none of it, what goes around comes around, and gave him the silent treatment. In the meantime, Archie had gathered his senses together, wondered how long before he got a new custodian.

The following day two more wheelmen in white coveralls arrived. They removed his front bumper, the winch, and his puncture proof wheels, then left him standing on wooden blocks. Archie remained in this undignified condition for some days. One morning a young wheelman, name of Spud, turned up with a recovery truck. He fitted some rather worn Land Rover wheels and tyres, winched Archie on board, and headed for Bucks, the place not the currency. The rest of the story dear reader you know. Archie hopes you enjoyed the ride.

THE END

Bonus

There follows a short story which Archie felt you might like, its called 1937, and is the story of a ten year old lad's exploits up to and during the first few years of the Second World War. This young chap is very entrepreneurial, and deals with the dangers and hardships with humour, and a light heart. I hope you enjoy it.

1937

It was 1937, I lived in a self sufficient family in Gosport, not far from the Royal Naval Dockyard in Portsmouth. Dad worked there as a Cabinet Maker, and very proficient he was too, having been a Royal Naval ships carpenter for many years. I was ten years old, brought up to be self sufficient, and always looking for a means of making a few pennies.

At that time, motor car ownership was for the very few, the roads were not full of cars vans and lorries. A good many trades people still used horse drawn vehicles to deliver their goods, the result of which was horse dung, just lying about, unclaimed and definitely unloved, particularly on hot summer days. Now there were a good many allotments near my home, almost everyone was out there growing a potato or cabbage, sometimes a mixture of both, with the odd carrot, parsnip or sprout thrown in. Now since all the locals were busy tilling the soil, I realised I could make my fortune supplying that most important of ingredients to a healthy vegetable patch, horse dung. I became a regular sight on the streets near my home, bucket and shovel in hand, performing my civic duty of cleansing the byways of aforementioned dung, which I then sold to the ever busy allotment holders for a handsome profit!

I was doing very nicely in the profit department, so well in fact that I had come to the attention of that most unfortunate of elements, the local thuggery, two thirteen year old boys, who thought my dung money would be more comfortable in their pockets than mine. Now these two were much bigger than me, I was after all the family runt, so that wasn't difficult. I was fortunate however, to have an older brother, he had taken me under his protective wing, knew he wouldn't always be about to look out for me, taught me to get in quick and fast, hit where it hurts. And that was exactly what I did, one of the thugs got a full dung bucket around the head, the other the handle of my dung shovel in the gonads! It worked a treat, neither of them seemed too well afterwards, I got to keep my hard earned dung money, and I gained two friends, well, sort of distant friends. The two thugs would always cross to the other side of the road when they saw me approaching, then wave a polite hello, most importantly, they never interfered again!

I began to realise that the dung business couldn't last forever, more and more cars buses and lorries were appearing on the road, there was less dung to be collected, and it was becoming dangerous, dodging between all those motors. I needed to branch out whilst still retaining the core dung business. My father being a cabinet maker, had many useful woodworking tools, and I was a quick learner, so I went into the business of refurbishing table tops, all wood, no formica or plastic, after all, it's the 1930's. This made a steady supplement to my dung money, and I smelt better into the bargain!

By the time I was twelve, my thriving business enterprises were becoming a full time occupation, or they would have done but for the interruption of schooling. This however was shortly to change, thanks to the sterling efforts of a certain fellow by the name of Mr Hitler. Now this fellow, Mr Hitler, has been criticized somewhat over the years, but there were some positives, which I feel should not be overlooked.

Mum had decided that I couldn't go to school anymore, since he, Mr Hitler, was dropping bombs near both my home and school, namely Portsmouth Royal Naval dockyard. Sometimes his aeroplanes would miss their chosen target, and Mum thought that I might get killed by a bomb being dropped on my school, so Mum banned me from going, hurrah! Instead of which I was to stay at home, then we could all get bombed and killed together, I suppose it would save on funeral expenses! So at the age of twelve years my schooling stopped, after all, I could read and write, mathematics was a doddle, what else did a chap need to know? For me it was all positives, I could continue without interruption my dung collection and table refurbishment business's, plus courtesy of Mr Hitler, I was now contracting out to build Air raid shelters for the neighbours, it was a win-win situation.

Then there was the entertainment, Mr Hitler's Stuka Dive Bombers, were making strenuous efforts to make sure that the docks at Portsmouth and Gosport ceased to exist. From my garden I could watch them going at it, then the Hurricanes and Spitfires would arrive and give the Stukas a right hammering. One day I was collecting dung with my apprentice George, he was only ten years old, but a good worker, didn't mind getting his hands dirty, and had a poor sense of smell! We would go around together picking up dung, the really sloppy ones George got. I told him, if you wanted to succeed, you had to start at the bottom, not literally you understand, wait till it hits the road, that's obvious isn't it? Anyway there we were, out on our rounds when the sirens went up, now I knew we were nowhere near the docks so no worry. No need to go crashing in on someone's shelter, particularly as George and I had done well on the dung that day, which meant we didn't smell too good, and wouldn't have been very welcome.

Next minute we heard the Dornier bomber getting closer, I knew it was a Dornier as it had an unusual engine note. Now I have subsequently been made aware of an expression used by our more flamboyant American cousin flyers, which is to 'plough the road'. Now I don't know if this particular pilot had an American relative, but he decided to re-surface the road upon which George and I were walking, and before you can re-surface a road you need to dig it up, or plough it, which the German pilot did, with his guns! Now George and I, we must be telepathic, as we both decided at the same instant, to have it on our toes as quickly as possible, away from the German bomber and his agricultural activities. This was all well and good, but our dung buckets were full, and our paths of escape happened to be in opposite directions, which rather throws my telepathic suggestion into some doubt. Well, we took each other out, down we went, dung and all. I landed on top of George as the Bomber flew over, at which point I jumped up as quickly as possible, George had got my bucket full pelt all over him, and he smelt bad, much more than he normally did! So with some dejection, and now with only partially full buckets, (both of us having a fair plastering of dung), we set off to our respective homes to get cleaned up. Mum was particularly upset when I arrived, as the local Catholic Priest was around for tea, and I walk in smelling like good and ripe dung! So courtesy of Mr Hitler I made a loss of earnings that day, and had to have a cold bath in the yard as I smelt so bad, and Mum had company.

However there is, or can be, a silver lining in the odd dark cloud, because the following day, Mr Jones the Postman called by. He told Mum how brave I was, as he had seen me jump on top of George to save him from being shot by Mr Hitler's pilot! Well that was it, I was a hero, at least for a few days I was, couldn't put a foot wrong. The truth of the matter is, although I like George very much, he is after all a very fine and loyal friend. There is no way in a million years I would have jumped on top of him, he was covered in the contents of both my, and his own dung bucket, and you would have had to be either very brave, or daft, to go anywhere near him!

Life continued along, with Mr Hitler's aeroplanes coming along and dropping bombs on the docks, then the Spits and Hurries giving them hell, I thought it was about time I joined in the fun. I was fourteen years old, Big Bro was on Aircraft Carriers, fixing up the fleet air arm aeroplanes. Dad, who had been on Dreadnoughts in the first big fight with Mr Kaiser, was now working in Portsmouth Dockyard. He was helping to fix up the Royal Navy ships that Mr Hitler was trying to blow up with his submarines. I decided that I would join the Royal Navy, I wanted to be an air gunner in the Fleet Air Arm, then I could join Big Bro on the Aircraft Carriers. I wasn't old enough yet, but I was sure I could convince the recruiter I was older, I had beefed up a bit with all of my business enterprises, and was sure I could pass for fifteen. So off I went to the Gosport recruitment office. They were really pleased to see me as press ganging had stopped some years earlier, I explained that Big Bro was on Aircraft Carriers, and I would like to join him as an air gunner in the Fleet Air Arm. My logic here was that I had no idea how to fly a plane, but I did have a good eye, I could knock a sparrow out of the sky at twenty yards with my best catapult!

I must say though that Mrs Churcher wasn't very impressed when I took the head off of her prize Sunflower, I thought it was a damn good shot at the time, at least thirty yards! Mum wasn't too happy when she heard about the sunflower, made me go and dig Mrs Churcher's allotment, and give her free dung! I thought at the time that digging the allotment was fair, but free dung as well? Collecting dung is a dangerous business, you have to dodge the motors which race about like they own the road, and then if your not too careful, some of the horses follow on when you think they have finished, and give you a dung hair conditioner! Not forgetting of course the horses big feet, some horses seem to be in a permanent bad mood, given half a chance, a well aimed horse kick can be very painful, put you off work for the rest of the day, it's very bad for profits. I often think that if Mr Hitler's bomb aimers were as accurate as many a

Gosport Dray Horse, he would have won the war already.

The recruitment fellow told me he was a Chief Petty Officer, which I thought was a good sign, as that was what Big Bro was. And it was, a good sign that is, because the recruitment fellow said I could join up as an Air Gunner, they had lots of vacancies as Air Gunners only lasted about three weeks. I thought that was very strange, how tiring could it be? They should try fixing tables and building air raid shelters for a living, then the recruiter fellow said they weren't tired, they were dead! Well I wasn't worried about that, if I could dodge those dray horse kicks, Mr Hitler's bullets would be no problem. I would get to join Big Bro, shoot down some of Mr Hitler's Bombers, and stop them trying to blow up Dad in his Dockyard, interrupting his tea breaks. As for the dead thing, No Chance, after all, George, (my business partner), he said I was bullet proof, and he would know, since I saved him from the bomber pilot with ploughing aspirations.

So off home I went, proud as punch, told Mum I was off to join Big Bro in the Royal

Navy. I thought she would be pleased, she wouldn't have to put up with me coming home smelling of dung, and damaging neighbours property with my catapult. Dad wouldn't have to put up with me borrowing his tools for my table refurbishment and air raid shelter building business. My only worry in the whole enterprise was George, he would have to manage the business on his own, he had worked hard, pretty much equalled me in the dung collecting department, and was coming on with the table refurbishment and shelter building. But it was a lot of work and we had a good customer base, I just hoped he could manage on his own. I told him he could join me as an air gunner when he was a little older, left him my catapult so he could get his eye in, then, DISASTER.

As soon as Mum heard my plans, she grabbed her coat, my birth certificate, and marched me back to the recruitment office. Mum gave the Chief Petty Officer a right good telling off, gave him one of her stares, and they could just about melt glass. She showed him my birth certificate, told him he should know better, sending young boys off to war! Well the Chief Petty Officer fellow was very apologetic, though he did go a bit red in the face, and gave me a really hard stare. But I was used to Mums glass melting one's, so he came nowhere, not even a close second, maybe a third or fourth. When we left I did hear some shouting, and what sounded like the big recruitment desk being given a sound beating, I thought I could go back later and offer to fix the table for a suitably reduced fee. When I mentioned it to George, he didn't think that was such good idea, and I could see that he did have a point.

That was it then, I'd have to wait another year before I could have a crack at Gerry, which was a bit worrying, it might all be over soon, and I would miss out! I also thought that three weeks wasn't very long, I mean in four weeks time it would be Christmas, Mum always put on a good spread, and I wouldn't have wanted to miss out on that, so maybe missing out on the air gunner job wasn't such a bad idea after all. When I got home and Mum had finished laying down the law to me, I sneaked out the back door, I had to find George, give him the good news.

I found him down the allotments, he was talking to Mrs Churcher, they had just agreed a price for shooting some of the local Squirrels which kept eating her sunflowers. George couldn't stop grinning when he knew I would be back for at least another year. I said he could keep my catapult as he needed the practice, also that for fear of missing the squirrels, and shooting off more Sunflower heads than the Squirrels were actually eating, we would trap them, and drown them in the water butt, I had heard that Squirrels don't swim too well!

The clock kept ticking and I hit fifteen years, I was particularly busy now, I could pretty much turn my hand to anything involving house repairs, which meant my services were much in demand helping the neighbours repair their bomb damaged property. I don't know what had happened to Mr Hitler's pilots, but their aim was definitely not what it used to be, after all, what good did it do, to blow up Mrs Churcher's prize sunflowers, or her runner beans for that matter. As a result, I would often find George down by the docks, dangling his worm, he said it was safer than being anywhere near the allotments, and the local fishmonger was always ready to buy his catch, which gave a nice additional income to his dung money. I had given up on the dung by now, left that side of the business to George, I had moved into cycles, in addition to property repairs of course.

Cycle repairs was a very lucrative business, they were a very popular mode of transport, all the dockers had one to get to work, and the dock gates at home time was like a tidal wave of push bikes. So I made a nice income from repairing Sturmey Archer three speed hubs, straightening mud guards and buckled wheels, even the odd paint job. In fact I had so much cycle work, I wondered what the dockers put in their tea that they couldn't ride in a straight line. Dad said that some of them would be hard pressed to cut a block of butter, never mind a mortise and tenon, so maybe that was the problem. And on the subject of butter, well there wasn't any due to rationing, which was due to food shortages caused by Mr Hitler's submarines blowing up our ships, and his bombers blowing up Mrs

Churcher's allotment. As for submarines, Dad said they were weapons of the devil, sneaking up on a perfectly serviceable ship, and blowing a hole in it with no warning whatsoever, it just wasn't gentlemanly behaviour. Dad said that anyone behaving like that deserved to lose the war, and the sooner the better as far as I was concerned, because Mrs Churcher has to be given a very wide birth every time her prize dahlia's were blown to atoms by one of Mr Hitler's cross eyed pilots. I just hope for their sake, that none of them ever crash their bomber anywhere nearby, I'm pretty sure there is an empty bean trench just waiting for them, either that or the water butt!

THE END

Author: cbm.caniwrite@gmail.com

This book may be purchased online at Amazon.

Printed in Great Britain
by Amazon